Office of the Dead

To Diane,

It was so nice to
meet you!

Bernard Suy, SMC

FREEBIE

Office of the Dead

Brother/Doctor Bernard Seif, SMC, EdD, IABMCP

Writers Club Press
San Jose New York Lincoln Shanghai

Office of the Dead

Writers Club Press
an imprint of iUniverse.com, Inc.

For information address:
iUniverse.com, Inc.
5220 S 16th, Ste. 200
Lincoln, NE 68512
www.iuniverse.com

ISBN: 0-595-17471-X

Printed in the United States of America

To Dorothy B. Sell, dear friend and Administrative Assistant, who has helped me to solve many a mystery.

CHAPTER I

Chill bit into the night air. Ice blue illuminated the room and washed over him like water color, making the midnight shadow on his jaw seem blacker and his eyes more hollow. He read from the computer screen out loud as he stood before it: "But if anyone leads astray one of these little ones who believes in me, he would be better off thrown in the depths of the sea with a millstone hung around his neck!"

"What in the name of God does that mean?" mumbled Detective David Gold.

"It's a quotation from the Christian Gospel," whispered a small pleasant voice from behind him. Dr. Chantal Fleur was called in on this case because she was a friend of the family and she was well aware that the detective didn't seem too comfortable with either of those facts. Her healthy looking chin-length brown hair bounced as she stepped back from Gold when he responded.

"I go to temple from time to time but must have missed that one," he stated, as his two hundred plus pounds turned toward the forensic psychologist behind him. Gold reverenced Christ as a great prophet. "I suppose Jesus is the one who said what's on the screen. You would know more about that than me, having gone through Catholic school."

"That's what one would think," she said, "but these days I'm pretty much of an agnostic. You know, not believing in or denying the existence of God. How about we turn on the lights and take a look around, Detective?"

"Sounds okay to me," he said half-heartedly. "Just don't touch anything or interfere with what we are doing in any way. My men are out at the pool guarding the crime scene and just waiting for the coroner to arrive and when he does, they will be all over the place in here."

Wailing and sobbing penetrated the office from outside and made them both reflexively look out the window toward the pool. Chantal left abruptly and rushed toward a lanky looking man slumped in a beach chair sobbing. In his mid-fifties, silver hair, completely distraught, he was the husband of the victim. An officer stood by him, inwardly hoping that his presence would be of some comfort, although the officer had nothing to say.

"John, let's go in the house and talk."

The man eventually rose from the beach chair as if in a trance and followed Chantal through the office, past the computer with the cryptic message, and into the early American living room. Behind them the garish red and blue lights of police cars and the rescue squad whirled, flooding the atmosphere with a harsh carnival mood. The coroner was there now, removing a woman's body from the pool. Even though it was only shortly after midnight, he looked unshaven and half asleep.

"When did you last see Beth, John?" asked Chantal in a voice as soothing and gentle as stringed music.

"About eight o'clock," he replied numbly. "I went over to my office to see patients this evening as usual and did a little paper work afterwards, returning here close to eleven. She was nowhere to be found. I couldn't even find a note from her and all I saw was that sentence on the computer screen. Is that some indirect type of suicide note?"

"I can't say yet, John, but we'll put it all together, I promise you. Right now we need to keep the focus on you."

"Dr. Fleur, can you come in here for a moment please?" Detective Gold boomed from the next room.

"Concentrate on some deep and easy breathing, John. Say the word 'one' or 'Jesus' each time you exhale. I'll be back as soon as I can."

She went into Beth's office. Gold's angry face met hers. His eyes bored holes through her skull.

"Please don't interrogate Dr. Johnson-Angelo. We want to keep him fresh for our people."

"I am just here as a friend, Detective; I'm not doing any interrogating. He is obviously in psychological shock and I am trying to minimize his symptoms."

"Sure you're not interrogating anyone, Doctor."

"Listen, I know that you don't like me, or perhaps it's just that you don't like my presence here. In either case, permit me to tell you that Beth and I went to grade school and high school together; we've been friends all our lives. We were split up for only a few years when she entered the Visitation Monastery in Wilmington, Delaware. The Order she entered was a cloistered one and we didn't see each other during my college years, but later, with the changes in the Church which came about through Vatican Council II, rules were relaxed and we got to see each other more frequently. She left religious life in the early seventies during a lot of the turbulence following the Council. She was progressive and her Order was not progressive enough for her. Beth worked hard and continued her education, getting an STD—that's a Doctorate in Sacred Theology."

The detective didn't seem impressed and responded smugly. "The way I hear it, this lady was not only too progressive for the Order she was in, but for the rest of the Church as well."

"Yes," Chantal countered with a tone of pride in her voice. "She had articles published in scholarly journals on everything from the Church's response to the poor, to the role of women in society and the Church. She was a scholar; she was a thinker. Beth was a prayerful woman. She made people uncomfortable sometimes, but that's because I think she was prophetic."

"Prophetic?" interrupted the detective. "Isn't that a Jewish concept?"

"The tradition continued into Christianity. Many people think that prophets are similar to fortune tellers, but actually they are women and men who believe that they have a message from the Lord for the rest of society. Most of the time we don't want to hear the message. They got their fortune teller reputation because in the Jewish Bible, at least, they would often say that if such-and-such a behavior or attitude wasn't changed, something negative would occur, and it often did."

"Doctor, why would this lady want to kill herself?"

"I don't think Beth did, Detective."

"Well," the investigator mumbled in a dubious tone, "when the coroner is through we'll know whether it's suicide or murder. Please stay away from everyone involved—okay?"

"I'll not disrupt your investigation, Detective, but my friend needs me at this time."

A blue uniformed police officer trying to mask his anxiety by an abrupt air and confident gait came into the room. He couldn't have been more than twenty-two years of age. "The coroner just left with the body, sir, and the team wants to come into the house now and gather evidence in here."

"Fine, officer, send them in." Eyeing Chantal, Gold continued: "On second thought, Doctor," he said, "maybe you can be of some help. Why not take the husband out for a little walk or something until we're through."

"Suits me fine, Detective."

CHAPTER 2

"Dr. Fleur's office, how can I help you?" said a crisp and efficient masculine voice on the other end of the telephone line.

"This is Detective Gold. I'd like to speak with the doctor or leave a message with her secretary."

"I'm her administrative assistant. I'll see that she gets any message you leave."

What is this world coming to, thought Gold. A man's voice as administrative assistant—what next? "Okay buddy, would you have her call me, it's police business and very important?"

"Certainly, Detective Gold, she should be finishing her current session with a patient any time now. He paused a moment before continuing. If you hold on a minute, her office door is opening and I think she'll be able to take your call shortly."

"Good, thanks a lot. Keep up the good work." And get a real job, he thought.

The forensic psychologist dictated some notes into a small tape recorder for a few minutes before picking up the telephone. "Good morning, Detective. Sorry to keep you waiting. If I don't dictate my progress notes immediately after a session I either forget to or they are

6

not as complete or helpful when I refer to them later. But enough of that. I hope you slept well after our grisly adventure last night."

"I sure did, Doctor. It wasn't any fun being at the crime scene with a dead body either," he responded with an ever so slight chuckle.

Is that an attempt at rapport via humor or simply an insult about being with me last night, she thought to herself. Chantal let the comment pass—for the moment anyway. Maybe her progress notes were not always the greatest, but her memory was!

"Dr. Fleur, I need your help. You seem somewhat knowledgeable about spiritual matters and Church related issues."

"Well, Detective, I minored in philosophy and went through Catholic school, and have—had—a friend whom I just lost who is—was—a former nun." Don't cry now Chantal, or this neanderthal will really think that you are a wimp.

"Sorry I didn't pick up on your pain last night, Doctor. I was given a gold shield when I became a police detective and an emotional shield when I became a cop. It was a loss for you, wasn't it?"

"Yes. Yes it was, Detective, but I try to be professional in situations like that. I'll deal with my mourning in my own way and on my own time." He received his emotional shield when he became a human being, Chantal mused.

"Our forensics people are trying to make sense out of the biblical quotation about leading little ones astray and having a rock tied around your neck and being thrown in the water if you do, and how this may relate to the suicide, murder, whatever it turns out to be."

"Detective, Beth was a theologian. She spent her life trying to draw closer to the sacred and to make sense out of it for the rest of us. Maybe she was struggling with that passage for some personal or academic reason. Does the coroner have any sense of whether her death was suicide—she paused before adding—or murder?" Both of those words choked Chantal as she said them. Breathing became difficult as she though of Beth underwater.

"It looks like murder at this point, Doctor. You see there was a rock carefully tied to a rope and then just as carefully tied to your friend's neck when we found her."

"Oh," in a choked voice, Chantal gasped, "My God, what a horrible death!"

Gold, belatedly remembering that the deceased was Fleur's friend, quickly suggested, "We can talk later if you like, Doctor. I know that you are busy."

"Oh no, that's all right. I'm just a little shaken. I'd really like to find out what happened and help in any way I can."

"Doctor, is there a priest you know or someone at the office building at the Diocese that we can bounce some of this off of to try to make sense out of it? He would need to be someone willing to spend some time with us processing all of this, someone with a flair for investigative work. Perhaps someone like yourself."

"I know people at the Chancery offices because I do some consulting for the Marriage Tribunal—you know—dealing with the petitions for marriage annulment of people married in the Catholic Church who've been divorced so that they can marry again in the Church. I've also done some psychological assessments on candidates going into religious life as Sisters or Religious Brothers, or becoming monks or nuns, for people—only men at this point—going into the Diocesan priesthood and diaconate, and for an ever growing number of lay people in ministry, so I have my connections, Detective, but I think there's another person that would better serve our needs."

"Here comes a thought—I bet he's a woman."

"Wrong, Kreskin. I went to graduate school and interned with him. He's a Catholic monk and clinical psychologist who specializes in behavioral medicine. He is, what shall I say, gentle but firm. That is, he has a gentle strength."

"Pardon my Judaism, but I though monks baked bread or made wine or something, and never talked."

"You are not alone, Detective, many Catholics stereotype them that way also. Some monastics continue to support themselves by baking bread or making wine, but there are many small monasteries and religious communities of men and women springing up anew since the Second Vatican Council when all the changes occurred in the Church. They are refashioning religious life and, in some ways, going back to its early roots and doing contemporary work to support themselves. They spend a good deal of time in silence, not as penance, but in order to have a quiet spirit which can hear the Lord and others better. My friend says it's like getting the static out of a radio so the message comes through more clearly. They don't have a TV; I guess that's why he used the image of a radio."

"My Aunt Elsie would have used the image of a Victrola. At any rate, you trust the guy and he's got good credentials, right?"

"The best, Officer."

"The best, Detective," he corrected.

"Detective, please understand that I don't want to 'bother your people,' to put it in your words."

"All right, all right, I deserve that. You're beginning to sound like my ex-wife."

"Tell you what, Detective, I have a few more patients to see and then a break from late afternoon till early evening. You could, if you like, pick me up around three. I can go over to the monastery where my friend is, with you, for a few hours. I'll put my mounds of insurance forms, managed care—or as many of us call it "managed uncare"—applications and treatment reports aside in honor of Beth."

"That sounds good, Doctor. You're a great guy—I mean person—I mean professional.

"Humph."

Bzzzzz.

CHAPTER 3

She slipped into his car looking surprising fresh after her busy morning and early afternoon. She smelled of "Loves Fresh Lemon" perfume—and he smelled of perspiration. "I'll be Chantal if you'll be Dave," she said, wondering what sort of response she would receive.

"That's okay by me as long as you don't mess with my people," he said, and they both smiled.

"Take route 209 South out of town. We'll be there in less than twenty minutes. We're headed out to the western part of Monroe County, the edge of the Pocono Mountains toward Brodheadsville."

"I don't remember any monastery out there," he said with a quizzical look. "What are you getting me into?"

"Remember that I said that this is new and small. The place was founded in 1987 by my friend."

"Hey, are you really sure he's legit? Give me his social security number and I'll put it through the police computer."

"Trust me on this one, Dave. In fact, the monastery was just listed in the *Scranton Diocesan Directory* and in the *Official Catholic Directory* for the first time last year. That's a real milestone for a young monastery. Francis was a member of a large international pontifical religious order for about twenty-seven years but always felt called to a more contemplative form of that life."

"I'm not sure what all this means but keep going, Chantal. I need all the enlightenment I can get."

"His original Order was made up of men with monastic habits on that spent most of their time running schools, parishes, and foreign missions and were about as talkative and active as most people except that they lived in communities and were celibate. Francis—that's his name—wanted more emphasis on silence and common prayer. I think they call the common prayer the Liturgy of the Hours these days; they used to call it the Divine Office. 'Office' implied a burden or duty; 'liturgy' has to do with the prayer of the People of God throughout the world, being united in praise and worship freely given. Francis is a positive person who reverences the power in words and symbols. He was also interested in a wholistic approach to the spiritual life, so his community has both men and women in it as well as a number of lay women and men associated with the monastery who live in their own homes but gather there for meetings, prayer, and the like."

"This sounds fishy, Chantal. Again, what are you getting me into?"

"No, Dave, honestly, you'll be pleasantly surprised. If you like, you can call the Bishop and check out his status. The Bishop approved the foundation of the monastery and it has been going very nicely. They work very hard to support themselves, keep a great deal of silence, and meditate quite a bit. They don't even have a TV—there would be little time for it anyway. Just don't look for a huge building and big arches and a bell tower and all of that, okay? If you want arches you had better head for McDonald's.

He's just about making it financially. They live on a shoe string. They seem happy and authentic. They have a few acres and a house with a few out buildings. I think the chapel's in a barn; they call the chapel an 'oratory' which is based on the Latin word *ora* or prayer and there's a guest house for men where a couple of monks live. The women in the community, that is the nuns, and the women guests on retreat stay in the main building. At least that's what it was like when I was out there about a year ago. Once in a while Francis and I collaborate on cases. As I said, he's a clinical psychologist and I'm a forensic psychologist and sometimes our backgrounds blend very nicely together. His specialty, actually it's a sub-specialty, is behavioral medicine. He treats a lot of people who have physical illness such as chronic pain, cancer, HIV/AIDS through the use of behavioral science techniques. He uses clinical hypnosis and a technique called 'Therapeutic Touch' quite often."

"This guy is sounding flakier and flakier to me Chantal. I am a city cop. I carry a gun and see the worst side of life everyday. I don't know anything about things like this."

"That's why I stayed with the Western things he does. Francis utilizes many Eastern healing techniques as well. He is especially fond of something called medical qigong, which is apparently spelled a number of different ways and includes slow physical movements, breathing exercises, as well as meditation. If I have things straight, medical qigong is not only a very ancient Eastern form of Therapeutic Touch but also an entire system of Chinese medicine."

"Are there any scientific studies to back this stuff up, Chantal?"

"Oh yes, just a search on the Internet can yield hundreds of studies with positive results, but many people, even well trained scientists, have their mind made up and are not open to looking at the data. Researchers and Western doctors are beginning to say, however, that

Chinese medicinal herbs are very powerful and must be used with caution, the way Francis does."

"Like I say, I know very little about such things."

"Well, Dave, there's one way to find out. You'll just have to meet the man."

Turning left off the highway and down a winding country road lined with leafy green trees on either side took us into a quieter and more serene inner and outer space. I was feeling lots of pain inside but trying not to show it to Dave or to anyone else. I really hadn't had time to let it all sink in. Beth was dead, probably murdered. As I quieted down, Dave, in contrast, seemed to get more and more restless. A simple red wooden sign with white lettering under the mailbox, probably handmade by one of the monastics, marked the driveway. "Salesian Monastery," it said. As we drove up the bumpy driveway, a large cross made out of old telephone poles, and impressive in its stark simplicity, welcomed us. We parked under it and walked toward the main building—a white, fairly large raised ranch house with a little barn red porch on the front.

"Brother Benedict. Brother Benedict." Chantal began to yell excitedly over toward a garden where a man in his late sixties with gray thinning hair and overalls was weeding the vegetables. He looked up, a little startled, or maybe a little annoyed, and finally a look of resignation came over his face. He got up quietly and walked toward the psychologist.

"Welcome, Dr. Fleur. I hope your presence here doesn't mean any trouble, or more work for our abbot. Please try to be as kind as you can to him."

"Okay Brother, it's a deal. Detective Gold, I'd like you to meet Brother Benedict, one of the members of the community."

"Pleased to meet you" went back and forth.

"A detective, huh," muttered the monk. "I suppose this one will be more trouble than ever! Abbot Francis is expecting you folks. Let me show you over to his office in the Hermitage."

We walked past the main house and, hidden away alongside the building, was a white mobile home. We opened the rear door which had a vinyl magnetic "Welcome" sign on it and then went into a small waiting area where we sat down on an old orange couch. The inside door to our left was closed and on it was a computer generated sign covered in plastic saying "Brother Francis de Sales, SMC, EdD." A stack of old *Catholic Digest* and *New Covenant* magazines sat on an end table, along with a few books and tapes that the monastery was peddling from their home and by mail order.

On the other side of the door lay a man in his late thirties stretched out on a massage table. He was dressed in faded grey gym shorts and his face radiated serenity. Shoulder length brown hair made him look like a left over from the sixties. His eyes were closed, as if in prayer. On one side of the table, a Thomas Merton looking man in his late forties wearing a light gray tunic and navy blue scapular with a hood lowered over his shoulders, the garb belted in the middle, was moving his hands slowly from head to foot a few inches above the physical body of the person on the table. The monk's intently listening face seemed to be registering feelings or perhaps some other type of information. On observation, it was difficult to discern if what the monk was receiving was coming from within him or through his patient. The abbot returned to the head and scanned down the body with his hands, lingering most especially around the heart. The patient turned on his side and the monk scanned the back from head to foot several times.

"Okay Mike, you can sit up whenever you like. Just take your time and make the transition gently and easily, opening your eyes gradually."

Mike just lay there for about two minutes, then opened his eyes and asked: "Dr. Francis, how did you know about the pain in my heart last time?"

"I can't completely explain it, Mike, but sometimes I get intuitive understandings when I do Therapeutic Touch. Some would call it a gift of the Holy Spirit, something unearned. At any rate, the information can be diagnostic of physical, psychological, or spiritual situations."

"That helps some. I felt electricity moving through me this time even more so than last and I saw some flashes of light," the patient said. "I had a pain in my heart that was very old and I knew I had no cardiac condition. But I now know what it is." He paused for a moment before continuing. "I've been estranged from my parents for some years. They were very neglectful and verbally abusive and I cut myself off from them. I need to do something with that but I'm not sure I know what just yet."

"Keep thinking about it Mike and maybe we can come up with some strategies next time. Then we'll get rid of that pain in your heart—okay.?"

"Not only okay, Dr. Francis, it's awesome!"

"See you next week at the same time Mike. I'm going out in the waiting room now to greet some people who want to see me. You can leave by the office door whenever you are ready. Take your time. By the way, Mike, I'd kill for your hair!"

"Thank you, and I'd kill for your intuition."

The abbot walked through the door and into the waiting room, shut the door behind him, and startled Dave by giving Chantal a big hug along with a kiss on her cheek. "It's so good to see you again, Francis. Thanks for taking time out of your busy day."

"It's a wonderful excuse to be able to see you, Chantal. This must be Detective Gold."

"Yes, ah, Brother, Abbot, Doctor."

"Francis is fine. I like 'Brother' best, but most of the time I wind up getting called 'Abbot,' so whatever works. A few call me 'Doctor.' The developmental researcher Erik Erikson says that we can experience an identity versus role confusion crisis as we move through life. I've been through it about six times now. How about if we walk around outside a little. It's a glorious day and I am sure that we all could use a little fresh air since our work coops us up a lot."

The other two nodded and followed Francis out the door. They walked past the main building. Brother Benedict quietly kept to his weeding as they walked down the driveway and out to the country road they had just driven in on. "Abbot, we are dealing with a possible murder or suicide of a woman theologian, an ex-nun, on whose computer was a Biblical quotation stating that those who lead little ones astray should have a rock tied around their necks and be thrown in the sea."

"Yes, Detective, Chantal told me that on the phone earlier today and she also told me that it was Professor Beth Johnson-Angelo who is the deceased."

"That's right, do you know her?"

"I've met her and her husband, Dr. John Johnson-Angelo, once or twice at professional conferences. I know her more through her writing in the theological journals than through the conferences, however."

"What exactly does that quotation mean, Abbot?"

"Well, Detective, I'm not a scripture scholar but my understanding is that Jesus was talking about how horrible it is to scandalize people."

"Eh, you mean like shock them?"

"Well in the Biblical sense, to scandalize means to act in such a way that you encourage other people to act in the same way and sort of lead them into sin. In my view of moral theology we are responsible for our own behavior, and that includes the behavior of one who gives bad example which would lead another into sin. For example, if your rabbi were having an affair and it became public and shocked others and weakened their faith and perhaps helped to lead them into sin he or she would be scandalizing them, and in the literal interpretation of this passage it would be better, without the forgiveness and mercy of God intervening, that this person be drowned."

You could see the computer whirling in the detective's head. Chantal's eyes were filling with tears and Francis continued walking on quietly for a moment just to let everybody be with whatever was going on within. Just then a car slowed down as it drove toward them. A smiling lady with curly hair turned silver by her children and grandchildren stopped and said hello to everyone. She told the Abbot she had been over to the office supply store and would get back to the typing. He thanked her and made a quick round of introductions, and Dotty drove off.

"Are Catholics always so pleasant?" the detective said.

"I don't think so, Detective, and I don't think Lutherans are always so pleasant either. Dotty's a Lutheran Christian and one of the most pleasant people I know, along with being the most realistic and Christian person as well."

Chantal appreciated the opportunity to lighten her inner feelings. "Well, here we are. A Catholic abbot who is some blend of progressive and very traditional, along with a Jewish detective, an agnostic psychologist, and a Lutheran secretary. All we need now is a Buddhist."

"Well, Francis smiled. I do have a good friend who is a Hindu Swami but let's save that for another day."

Detective Gold just raised his eyes and wondered why he came, grateful for the fact that at least the abbot had a woman for a secretary.

They had walked to the end of the bright country road and were near Route 209, the main highway. The trio turned around to walk back.

"Here's my hypothesis, Detective," said the abbot. "Beth either felt she led people astray by her writings and took that Biblical passage more literally than most of us would and killed herself, or there's some psychopath out there who felt the same way and did it for her."

"Now we're getting somewhere Abbot. Thank you."

Chantal couldn't quite absorb what she was hearing. "How would anybody, why would anybody kill Beth," she thought out loud. "I think what you need, Detective, is a psychological autopsy to help you."

The detective shrugged and said: "Me and behavioral science never got along real well. We have the police shrinks to help us from time to time and they're always over-booked and underpaid as it is. Besides, what cop would want to let others know he's a little crazy."

"I'll do the psychological autopsy, Chantal offered, if that won't be interfering too much, detective."

"Well, I suppose it won't hurt anything, if you can tell me what it involves?"

Chantal described the process of clinical interviews with people close to Beth—friends, relatives, associates, analysis of her writings, her behavior, her schedule, everything that would reflect on who this person was and whether there was some motivation to take her own life or not.

"Her husband's in pretty bad shape, Francis. I wonder if you'd be able to see him for a few sessions to help him out. I'm just a little too close to the situation for that."

"It would be my pleasure, Chantal. Have him call the monastery and we'll work it out."

They had strolled to the beginning of the driveway and the sound of a bell was heard pealing over by a little barn. "It's about time for our Evening Prayer or Vespers, which is the older and more traditional term for this part of our Liturgy of the Hours or Divine Office. If you don't need me for anything else I'll go in and sing for my supper. It's my turn to play the keyboard this week so I suppose that I've got to make an appearance. I don't want to lead any of these little ones astray by not showing up and giving bad example. You're welcome to join us if you like, folks."

"Maybe I'll take a raincheck on that Abbot, especially since I'm not Christian."

"That's fine, Detective, but what we'll be singing are psalms from the Psalter of the Jewish Bible along with a Christian reading and some prayers for our world at large. Thank you for passing them on to us. The psalms are the backbone of our liturgical prayer."

"Interesting, I didn't know you guys were into that. I thought our Bible was passe."

"Not only is it not passe, my friend, but it is the foundation of our faith. We are grateful."

Brother Benedict, now in his blue and grey habit, nodded in our direction and walked into the oratory. There was a woman in a modified nun's habit also in view of the trio. She wore a simple grey tunic and navy blue scapular with a matching blue veil which covered the back of her head. The monastic woman, or nun, could be seen through a window sitting at her choir stall. A younger man also in a grey tunic but wearing the white scapular of a novice rather than a blue one, was walking down the steps of the main building, and another nun was walking not far behind. Chantal watched Dave. His eyes took everything in and recorded it. They drove slowly out of the driveway, pensive and silent.

"Why the cross?" asked Dave.

"Oh, you mean that big cross of telephone poles—that was constructed with the compliments of Commonwealth Telephone company."

"No, I don't mean that one, Chantal. I mean the one around the Abbot's neck. Nobody else had one on."

"It is a monastic tradition, as I understand it. The Abbot or the Abbess is the spiritual leader of the community and wears a cross to symbolize that. Kind of like a Bishop does. A Bishop runs a Diocese and wears a cross as a symbol of that. And like a Bishop who has a staff or crozier or shepherd's crook, or whatever you would like to call it, the Abbot or Abbess has one as well, except that his or hers is often simply a plain wooden staff as opposed to something that might be made of metal and more ornate."

"What does he specialize in again, Chantal."

"Behavioral medicine, Dave. It's the medicine of the future. I don't understand all of it but I know he uses clinical hypnosis and self hypnosis training to enhance the function of patients' immune systems, to relieve the side-effects of chemotherapy, to reduce anxiety, to help women deliver babies with hypnosis rather than medications, situations like that."

"Ah, that's interesting work for a monk. I still think he ought to be making jelly or bread or something." After a few moments thought, Gold asked,

"What about this Therapeutic Touch, Chantal? I heard people talking about something called Reiki. Is it related to that?"

"I believe that it is Dave. I really don't know too much about it. It's something that was developed by a nurse practitioner named Dr. Dolores Kreiger and has been taught all over the world. I understand that it lowers blood pressure, it stops babies from crying, it speeds up the healing of wounds, it raises the hemoglobin level in the blood. Some people report getting intuitive information of a diagnostic nature by doing Therapeutic Touch on their patients."

"What do you mean, like, if they have a bad liver or something?"

"Yes, Dave, it can be physical situations, but emotional or spiritual things are also sometimes reported to be revealed to the practitioner."

"Chantal, this is getting weirder by the minute."

"I know; I thought I'd save the best for last."

"Does your friend get any of this 'intuitive information' as you call it?"

"I'm pretty sure he does although he's very quiet about it. Some of it is because of confidentiality and some of it is because I don't think he wants to come across like a quack to the scientific community, or like a heretic to the spiritual community. I don't think he's either."

"We'll see, Chantal. Maybe he's both."

Chapter 4

"Dr. Johnson-Angelo's office," she said into the phone. "No, I'm sorry, the doctor won't be in today. We're in the midst of canceling all of his appointments. I'm sorry, ma'am, he didn't say when he would be back. Let me put you on hold for a minute." The secretary pressed a button on the telephone and it rang in John's home. He let it ring a few times and then despondently reached his hand over and picked it up. "Doctor, this is Gayle. Can I tell your patients when you'll be returning? I really don't mean to disturb you but…"

"You can tell them anything you like Gayle. I just can't seem to get it together."

"Doctor, if you don't mind me saying—maybe working will be a good distraction for you. You know how you come to life when you're around your patients."

"Who are you to tell…?," and then he stopped himself. "I'm sorry, Gayle, I'm not mad at you, I'm mad at all of this. We've worked closely for many years and I suppose I need to trust your judgment on this. I'll try to be over there by noon. Just sort of take care of me and guard me from the crowd if I need to get out again."

"Sure, Doctor, please come over by noon." She got back on the phone with the patient and said, "Come in about noon. We might be able to fit you in."

"Well," thought Gayle, "that's great. At least we didn't have to refer this one to another group." She meditated on what a difficult specialty family medicine is. You have to be all things to all people—part physician, part psychologist, part spiritual director—and try to keep your fees low. It was not even eleven in the morning and already the office was full. A few phone calls from Gayle had gotten the word around and everyone was coming in to have their ills treated. John let himself in through the back door, his stomach knotted like a day old pretzel.

Who doctors the doctor, he thought as he felt himself being overwhelmed by the depression once again. Gayle heard him in his office and tapped on the door quietly. He even more quietly whispered "come in." She went in with a stack of phone messages and read the top one to him.

"Abbot Francis from the Salesian Monastery would like you to give him a call, Doctor."

"Can't you just give him an appointment for me, Gayle?"

"I don't think he wants to be your patient. I think he's reaching out to you."

"Well, whoever he is I've got too much to do to get involved with him. Please try to take care of those other messages as best you can."

"I will, Doctor, and I'll let the first patient come in now." In walked a healthy looking middle-aged woman who had diabetes and was there for a check-up. John felt annoyance at seeing her and knowing there were other patients out there waiting to drain him as well, but he swallowed it and began examining his patient. By the end of the session he was lost in her case and feeling somewhat improved. His work was like anesthesia for him. At five-thirty Gayle came to the door with a tray of fast food and told him she would hold the crowd off until six. He smiled the first weak smile he was able to manage in several days. Gayle came in to pick up the tray shortly before six and without warning started to sob.

"I'm sorry, Doctor Angelo. I've tried to be strong but I'm sorry for you and I'm sorry for your wife and I'm just plain sorry. I'm happy, happy that you're here and happy for what you've done to help me and please let's just get on with our work."

John held back his temper and felt the sting of the real issue—the pain underneath his anger. Trying to sound light, he said:

"Gayle, you know that when I married Beth I put her last name in front of my own. I want now more than ever to keep that name. Why would you suddenly drop it? Besides, you know that you don't need to call me Doctor anything. John is fine."

"Forgive me, Doctor. I meant no disrespect to Professor Johnson-Angelo, or to you. I'm just trying to keep it together as best I can and regressed to what I called you when I first started working for you. It won't happen again."

CHAPTER 5

Chantal's patients were giving her strange looks ever since her name appeared in the paper mentioning her as the consulting psychologist on the murder of Professor Beth Johnson-Angelo. She, in fact, was giving Detective Gold strange looks ever since he asked her to take on that role for him. Maybe Beth had performed her first miracle!

Even though Chantal did see some people for psychotherapy for a variety of disorders, she spent most of her time preparing for court, or actually being at the courthouse, as an expert witness on investigations dealing with the psychological competence of people who were involved in accidents, compensation claims, or other legal matters. She tried to keep Fridays free for paper work and her office patients and today found that one person after the other would bring up the case that presently saddened her so deeply.

If there was a God, why did he/she let this happen? Why did God let this happen to someone like Beth? Beth spent her life devoted to God, devoted to coming to a deeper understanding of God for herself and for others. Beth put her head and employment on the chopping block time and again in the theological stances she took and now, by her own hand, or someone else's, was dead.

The pathologist's autopsy report found no evidence of a struggle. Church officials had recently been trying to silence her, but that had been going on for years. John loved her passionately even though he was jealous of the memories she had about religious life and some of the friends, in and out of her former religious community, who drew her energy and emotion away from him at times.

Chantal couldn't concentrate. She skipped lunch again, skipped dinner again, and drove over to John's office. Gayle looked up appreciatively as Chantal entered.

"Let me see if I can slip you in between patients, Doctor Fleur. I know you're in between patients yourself." Before long, the door opened and a woman and her daughter stepped out, the daughter holding an inhaler to help her with her asthma attacks. Everyone looked up anxiously waiting to be called but Gayle jumped up and was at the door before people knew what happened. In a moment she was ushering Chantal into the doctor's office.

"How are you doing, John?" she asked.

"I manage okay when I'm with my patients but otherwise it's pretty horrible."

"Have you talked to Abbot Francis, John?"

"No, I haven't, I guess I'm mad at God as well as everybody else."

"He's not God. He met you about a year ago at a conference on the psychological aspects of medical care."

"Oh right, I thought the name sounded familiar. Does he do something other than being an abbot?"

"Yes, John," she said compassionately. "He's a clinical psychologist, and a very fine one. That's why he wants to see you. I asked him to. He's reaching out to you in your pain."

"Well, I'd rather keep my wound closed for now, Chantal, but I appreciate both of you thinking of me."

"Okay, John, I don't mean to be a meddler. I just wanted to encourage you. I know you're busy so I'll leave you now. Call if you need me."

"Thank you, Chantal, I really appreciate it."

In a moment Chantal was gone and a little baby with a dangerously high fever was on the examining table before him.

CHAPTER 6

"Please come in, Brother Matthew. Make yourself comfortable."

"Thank you Abbot Francis. I'll keep working on the make yourself comfortable part."

The Abbot smiled. "I can understand that. You've only been here about a year and are just beginning your two-year novitiate. It takes a while for us really to settle into the monastic life. I'm still working on it after more than thirty-five years."

"Well, then, I guess there's hope for me."

"Oh sure, lots of hope," said the Abbot with warmth and encouragement in his voice. "By the way, Brother, are you still taking your Chinese medicinal herb formula, *An Mien Pien*?"

"I do when I remember Abbot Francis. It helps me to sleep and keep those feelings of panic away."

"Good, but we need to do our inner work too. You're soon to have a birthday, aren't you Brother Matthew?"

"That's right Abbot Francis; in a few days I'll be twenty-four."

How much he's packed into his young life, thought the Abbot. College for computer programming, engaged and almost married, and a year or two checking out the Catholic Traditionalist Movement—a

splinter group of the Roman Catholic Church that represents the opposite end of the spectrum from Beth's point of view. And his singing
voice! He sounds like an angel in the oratory, such a contrast to what is
going on within him.

"Brother, you know you can come and talk with me any time."

"Yes, Abbot Francis, I understand that. But you're so busy; I hate to
take up your time. And really, I haven't had any major problems in a
while. At first the silence was pretty intense here and I was lonely, but
I've come to terms with a lot of that—and the nightmares are stopping,
which, I suppose, is a sign of healing."

"It can be, Matthew, or it can be a sign of repression. We need to
make sure that your choice of not only this lifestyle, but of your
response to the changes in the Church since Vatical Council II is something which is genuine for you. You were pretty wrapped up in the traditionalist movement and if that's where you need to be, so be it. But if
you're here, you need to be here heart and soul." The novice's large sky
blue eyes filled with fear and the energy in the room felt as of the curly
auburn hair on the top of his head was standing straight up.

"Are you asking me to leave, Abbot Francis?"

"No. No, not at all. You're a fine person and a real asset to our community. I just want you to do what is truly in your heart. The nightmares are an indication that you need to listen to something that you
have not been listening to."

"But I told you they've stopped—pretty much."

"That may be the case, but have they been replaced with insomnia?"
With that, the novice monk began to sob from his soul. "Matthew,
you're falling asleep in the oratory and even at meals. You've lost a con-
siderable amount of weight and you don't look happy. How about writing down your nightmares and we can process them? Catch whatever

you can of them, even if it's only fragments. Dreams are something like DNA; you only need a minute sample to be able to break the code."

"I'm afraid to do that, Abbot Francis, because then you'll really think I'm crazy and throw me out on my ear."

"Brother, I can't say what I'll think because I haven't seen them yet, but I do know that I've dealt with many, many people regarding their nightmares and it has been a life-giving and freeing experience. So please try to trust the Lord who seems to have lead you here. It may be that God is trying to enlighten you, to raise your awareness to some conflicts within you so that you can be at peace about them and not waste all your energy burying issues. Only in the place of healing do we dare to show our wounds. Any wounding you feel will bring new life. That was the experience of Jesus. What do you say?"

"Well, I suppose that my head's going to be completely covered with bumps if I let it fall on my choir stall one more time during Liturgy of the Hours and I'm going to burn my nose if I fall into my soup again," he laughed and blew his nose and coughed, still trying to mask his tears of fear and resignation.

"Sleep, Matthew; let the nightmares happen and write them down. Jot down some old ones too if you remember them and we'll talk again in a few days. Now go with God's peace and blessing."

"Thank you, Abbot Francis, for giving me a chance."

"And thank you, Matthew, for giving God a chance."

CHAPTER 7

"So what's with the male administrative assistant, Chantal? Is this some type of a feminist thing or perhaps a nineties statement?"

She sighed. "No, David, it's simply the case of a young man who's struggling in graduate school at the university and I am part of his work/study program. In other words, he gets paid to help me and it gives him a bit of experience in the area of clinical psychology. He's here twenty hours a week and, by the way, does a super job."

"Any problems with ethics or confidentiality thus far, Chantal?"

"No, Carl seems very ethical and we had a long talk about confidentiality and privileged communication. He's been trained at the university but if there are any slip-ups it's on my license and I'm the one that will be in trouble. It's an occupational hazard, Dave."

Dave scratched his head. "What's the difference, if any, between confidentiality and privileged communication?"

"Confidentiality is an ethical obligation whereby a professional is required to keep his or her dealings with a client or patient secret, as it were. Privileged communication, on the other hand, is granted to licensed professionals such as clinical psychologists, physicians, and religious leaders and essentially makes them immune from divulging information about others in a court of law. There are some limits to the privilege, for example information about child abuse. In fact, we are mandated to report that even if we are not in court."

"I think I got it! Some states don't license certain professionals, for example, counselors. So they would be bound to ethical confidentiality but not have privileged communication before the law."

"Exactly, my friend. Psychologists are licensed in all fifty states and the District of Columbia and have privileged communication in one form or another in all jurisdictions."

"Moving from the world of the abstract to reality, Doctor, how's that psychological autopsy going on Beth?"

"It's just about completed; I'm going over to the monastery to talk to Francis about it tomorrow and to get his input."

"Mind if I tag along, Chantal?"

"No, Dave, as long as you don't interfere with my work! How's that for reversing the roles?"

"Well, not too bad, especially since we are on our way out to dinner under the guise of working, and I am getting the distinct impression that we might almost be enjoying one another's company."

"Don't push it, Detective."

The ambience was delightful, complete with checkered tablecloths, perfect bread sticks, a friendly but not overly friendly waiter, and a bottle of wine. "I really like Italian food, Dave. Thanks for suggesting this place. We'll probably get good service because your dark Mediterranean complexion makes you look Italian."

"I think we'll get good service because you're beautiful. But don't mind me, I think it's the oregano talking."

"You know, Dave, I think I must have been Italian in a past life. This place really is fun."

"Past lives, Chantal, do you really believe in that?"

"Oh, I don't know what I believe. That was just a little attempt at humor."

"Are you sure you don't really believe in that? At times you seem pretty gullible to me."

"Gullible? What's that supposed to mean, Detective?"

"Oh, I don't know. You tend to take people at their word, you know, you believe most people when they tell you something."

"Well, don't you, Dave? How about when you said you were beginning to like me, or when you mentioned that you thought I was pretty. Was that true or was I being gullible?"

"You'll never know, Doctor."

"So, I'm gullible and now you're playing mind games with me. What else do you want to do to ruin our evening?"

"Me ruin our evening? You're the one who's getting cranky."

"Cranky? Dave, you've just insulted me a couple of times over. Who wouldn't be a little perturbed?"

"A little perturbed? You're annoyed, I can tell it, just like my ex-wife, what a woman! Couldn't look at her crooked without her bursting into tears and becoming angry."

"Well, Dave, I'm not a tear-burster. I'm strictly anger. Do you have some unresolved issues still brewing with your ex, Dave?"

"No, why do you ask?"

"Well, you brought her up a couple of times and it's a pretty intense feeling level emitted when you bring her up."

"Don't get shrinky with me. We're here to have fun, not to pick each other's brain."

"Dave, you're the one who started the mind games. Maybe it'd be better if I left now, okay?"

"Suit yourself." Chantal stood up and started to walk toward the door. A waiter came over and asked if everything was all right. She said that everything was fine. "I'm just getting to know someone whom I believe I probably don't want to know. Thank you."

She was out on the street, hailed a cab, and was back home before Dave had even left the restaurant. Chantal didn't turn to the junk food she was tempted to binge out on but worked out on her treadmill instead and followed that with a long, hot shower. She was on the couch in her robe and watching the late news when the intercom buzzer to her apartment rang. A little startled, she got up and pressed the talk button and asked who it was.

Dave's voice boomed through the speaker saying: "It's a jerk with a pizza. He looks Italian, but he's not, and if you let him in he won't bring up his ex again or play mind games."

"Did you bring any wine?" she hollered back.

"Maybe, but I'm not going to bribe you. I'm not just another pretty face."

"Okay, handsome, I'll buzz you in." Pizza on TV trays with a little Anne Murray music in the background—what could be more delightful? "When we both apologize, we might try to figure out what it is that irritates the other. Then again, maybe the hour is too late for that sort of heavy conversation. What do you think, Dave?"

"I'm too tired, Chantal. I'm just happy we're talking. I'm not the shrink but I think it has something to do with our backgrounds and this case."

"Oregano," she said with a twinkle in her eye.

CHAPTER 8

"Come in, Doctor Johnson-Angelo. What finally gave you the inner freedom to trust me enough to come over?"

John looked at the abbot with mixed emotions. "If you want to know the truth, it's the fact that you have read my wife's work."

"Oh, yes, I've read it and I respect it. She's thorough, she's sound and she's passionate about her love of God and the Church. I am grateful that I was able to meet her and that she lives on through her writings."

"You look a little confused, Doctor, can I help?"

"Well, it's just that you're sitting here dressed like someone from the Middle Ages and yet you are in touch with the latest in contemporary theologians and not intimidated by the questioning attitude of people like my wife and others. What are you—liberal or conservative?"

"Well, Doctor, I guess I can't be diagnosed all that easily. Let me put it this way. I try to live by the *Tao* and even that is an undefinable concept and experience."

"I know this much about *Tao*, Abbot, it has something to do with the coming together of all creation, the Yin and the Yang, the masculine and the feminine, darkness and light, opposites coming together and complementing one another, 'synthesis,' 'individuation,' words like that."

"Very true, Doctor, and all of that within the context of energy, life, God, grace, however you want to name it, him, her."

"Well, Abbot, all of that meant something to me until about two weeks ago when my wife was murdered and now I'm not sure what makes sense. What had been existing peacefully together in my inner life has been scattered to the four winds. Beth gave her life completely to God in one way or another for well over fifty years and this is what she gets in return. I give my life to helping other people and am left alone to do it."

"John, if I may call you that, life is obviously unfair. You know that very well on a head level from your work as a physician, as I do being a clinical psychologist and spiritual director. If you can assimilate that simple statement about unfairness on a heart level, you will experience the wonder of the *Tao* within your deepest darkness."

"That sounds beautiful and poetic, Abbot, but I hurt."

"I know you do. You've got to. I think maybe you hurt not only emotionally but also physically."

"What do you mean, Abbot?"

"Well, my specialty is behavioral medicine. Did anyone tell you that?"

"No, they didn't. I thought that you were a clinical psychologist."

"I am that, but I deal a lot with physical problems using behavioral science approaches. I don't mean this to brag, but I know that you understand what a post doctoral diploma, or board certification as it is sometimes called, is. In fact, my guess is that you are board certified in family medicine."

"That is correct, Abbot."

"Well, I fulfilled the mandatory five years of post-doctoral experience in behavioral medicine, obtained the necessary letters of recommendation from professionals in the field, submitted a video-taped and transcribed work sample to the board for analysis, passed the comprehensive examination and am a diplomate in behavioral medicine of the International Academy of Behavioral Medicine, Counseling, and Psychotherapy.

What a mouthful! Again, I offer this just to help to establish some credibility with you, John, and to build a little professional rapport. Also, the spiritual side of healing is much simpler and open to us all, no special schooling needed. And now that I've told you a little about my background and philosophy, it will be up to you to work with me or not as you so choose. I have more patients than I can manage as it is. I would be happy to work with you but am not desperate for work by any means."

"I appreciate your honesty, Abbot, and will try to keep an open mind. A physician playing God under these conditions just wouldn't work, now would it?" A faint smile.

"One therapeutic treatment which I use combines spirituality, physics, and psychology and is called by a variety of names and taught in a variety of ways and cultures but is something that many people would call Therapeutic Touch."

"I've heard of that. Some of the nurses were using that at the hospital and it had interesting results. But I must say that it just sounds like hocus-pocus to me."

"Well that's fine, John. Let it be hocus-pocus as long as it helps us. Here comes the kicker, John. I sometimes get an intuitive sense when I scan a person with my hands and once in a while when it's very profound I don't even need to scan, and that's why I know your whole GI tract is out of whack. You've had the runs for days; you've been vomiting, your electrolytes are off, and you want to stay that way."

"What do you mean, I want to stay that way? Who are you to tell me what I want and don't want? He paused to let his anger subside. "I'm sorry, I don't mean to be so angry, Abbot. And I was so taken aback that I missed the part about asking you how you knew all of that. Are we still friends?"

"Of course, John. One of the first things I learned as a psychotherapist was that people often unconsciously transfer negative, and sometimes positive, perceptions from their past on to the therapist. The same is true with a physician and possible for anybody for that matter. We can become like a projector screen, better yet a lightening rod, for our patients. Sometimes I am the mother who abused them, the nun who took a special interest in them in grade school, and on and on. As the patient works through the often intensely powerful transferred feelings, he or she becomes free from distorted unconscious reactions and learns to respond more and more in freedom to life events. I guess you can tell that I was a teacher in a past life, so to speak."

"My father used to read our minds, tell us what we were thinking or feeling, and I hated it. This little discussion has made me more aware of why I am so sensitive when people do even a little bit of that. You have helped me already."

"The power to heal is within you, John. I am like a midwife; my role is to bring that new life out of you."

"What a beautiful image, Abbot. Now can you tell me how you knew about my physical symptoms?"

"Actually, I'm not sure how I knew and I didn't mean to confront you too harshly about wanting to keep your symptoms, but I think it's something we need to think about. As a physician, you know there's a payoff to being sick at times and I believe that your physical and emotional illnesses are giving you some type of payoff. Why don't you go home and ponder about what the payoff might be and then come back and maybe we can do some Therapeutic Touch? Okay, John?"

"Well, I don't know. I'll have to think about it. I truly appreciate your thinking about me but I just think I might like to leave things the way they are."

"I'm sure you would, John; I'm sure you would."

John left the office and walked toward his car. Passing a nun in her 40s on her way into the main building he thought that she looked vaguely familiar to him. The nun seemed to turn away and pick up her pace when he looked toward her.

CHAPTER 9

The Abbot sprinkled each of us with holy water as we left the oratory after night prayer. The community entered into its grand silence until after breakfast the next day. Then simple silence would pick up and we would be able to talk for lesser reasons, for example, a need during work, or out of charity to a visitor or another monastic. During grand silence only the greatest emergency would allow us to talk. There was always an intensity about the night.

Brother Matthew made it up the steps to his room in the men's guest house and barely got his belt off and scapular up and over his head and off when he flopped on to his bed and went into a profound sleep, still in his grey tunic. Before long, the dream began again. A mysterious woman approached who was angry with him. She wanted him to talk with her, spend time with her, get to know her, like her, love her—but he would have none of this. He asked her to go away. She became indignant. They struggled. He found himself trying to kill her. She would never die—almost, but not quite. Then, filled with the horror of what he was doing, he would scream and shake violently and wake up or be awakened by Brother Benedict who certainly did not approve of this behavior, especially in a novice.

CHAPTER 10

In a cozy room lined with books—too many books for the shelves—a meeting was being held. The community creatively used just about every corner of the building and every inch of space but continued to need more room. Most of the volumes were about the spiritual life, some of them ancient looking, others just off the press. Some books contained the wonders of philosophy and psychology. All of them were used as food for the soul. A library truly reflects the people who own it, especially when the people are striving to find their reflection in one another and in the Sacred.

Chantal, David, and Francis sat at an old oak table. Chantal was delivering the results of her psychological autopsy to this small but august committee. David's temper was starting to flare.

"You mean to tell me that you knew that Abbot Francis treated Beth in the late seventies and you never told me?"

"Yes, David, I couldn't get hold of you during the week and last night was so rocky that I just didn't get to bring it up, but I knew I'd be telling you today so where's the harm?"

"The harm is that this is material, Chantal, that I could have had in mind as I continued on with this investigation and am only now getting it."

"I only found out about it the other day, David."

The man and woman looked at Francis as he began to speak. "We have an ethical issue here. I treated someone in confidentiality and under the privileged conditions, supported by civil law as well as canon law. It was shortly after she left religious life and was floundering around. I was an intern at a hospital where she was an out-patient and didn't even know if I could get the records until a few days ago. I did get the records. Chantal has them now. We each have before us a copy of the psychological autopsy. How about we move on from there, presuming the good will of everyone involved?"

"Okay by me Francis, if I may call you that."

"That's fine with me, Dave."

"By the way, Francis, let me lighten the atmosphere a little and ask you a question. Does that title Abbot come from Abba, the Aramaic word for daddy?"

"Yes it does, Dave, you're right on target. I really consider myself a brother to the Brothers and Sisters here and that is why I tend to call myself that, but I do answer to 'Abbot' and 'Doctor' and 'Brother' and once in a while from Catholics 'Father,' although that's not really accurate."

Chantal wondered out loud: "Why from Catholics?"

"Well, Chantal, most Catholics are so used to priests that when they see a man in a Church-related position they stereotype him into being a priest whether he is one or not. My call is to monasticism, the vowed life of contemplation, silence, and the overflowing of that into service for others. I have monastic vows, that is my whole vocation from God and consecrates me to God. Baptism does that in many ways for all Christians."

"I understand that, Francis. I remember when we were in graduate school and even more as interns you were on the brink of making this decision to found the monastery. You always seemed restless in your original community. You stated that most of the men were priests. Even though you admired many of them and some of them were close friends and continue to be, the emphasis was not on the vowed life, it was more on priestly ministry."

"That's exactly right, Chantal, and that's good for some people, but I know what I'm called to and here I am with bills and broken water pipes and all that goes with it. We need to be honest to our primary call or those demons we call symptoms result."

"As fascinating as this all is, Dave interjected, we'd better get to the heart of why we're here."

"Very well. I've written up a report," Chantal said," and you each have one for review, I will point out a few of the highlights at this time. I'll simplify the matter by cutting out background data with which we are already familiar and get right to the heart of the matter. Here we go. Her husband, her friends, her colleagues tell me in every possible way that Beth was not suicidal. She was experiencing hassles and struggling to live and be with what she felt called to be, but had been living with that kind of stress for many years now."

"Why do I sense a 'but' coming?" questioned Dave.

"Because about fifteen years ago when Francis treated her she did exhibit some suicidal ideation. Many people do now and then and it passes fairly easily. Francis gave me a psychological assessment report that he did on Beth when we interned. He had a very competent supervisor who reviewed it and co-signed the report, which is mandatory for a supervisor. Beth was coming to terms with something. She had shed the identity of being a religious after having worked so hard for change and new life for her community, and now was struggling to make it on her own, and in the most challenging arena—by becoming a theologian, which had been largely a man's domain and a priestly domain. Here was this laywoman struggling to make ends meet financially, coming to clarity with her genuine identity and call and terrified about all of it."

"Some people call it a sort of Zen madness," Francis offered. "St. John of the Cross, the famous Carmelite mystic and contemplative, teaches that at some point all of our images of God, the afterlife, and ourselves, can collapse. We experience great disorientation and only then do we become truly who we are and know God for what God is. This is where Beth was. It was not a chronic mental illness. It was a profound rite of passage."

"Pardon me for saying this, Doctors," Gold pragmatically offered, "but my boss is claiming that this lady theologian killed herself." With that Dave suddenly jumped up startling both Chantal and Francis and said, "Can I use the phone?"

"Is something the matter, Dave?," Francis said. "You jumped up awfully quickly without any apparent reason and we're not sure why."

"Oh, that, it's the beeper in my pocket. I have it on vibrate so when somebody is trying to get hold of me I feel the thing vibrate, even through the flab."

"Oh, I get you," Francis stated. "When I was an intern, we had the old-fashioned kind that simply made noise. And yes, there's a phone over there. Feel free to use it. Would you like some privacy?"

"No, that's all right." Dave punched in a number quickly and was overheard saying: "Yes, yes, where, how long ago, I'll be right there." He hung up, turned to his two colleagues and said: "There's been a death, I've got to go."

"Is there anything we can do?" Chantal said.

"No, I don't think so. On second thought, maybe you can pray. It's in a religious place."

"Where's that? Francis asked.

"A place you may know of, the Center for Traditional Catholicism. One of the priests there was either murdered or committed suicide."

CHAPTER 11

"The coroner's here, Detective, but of course we didn't touch anything; we were waiting for you to arrive."

"Good thinking. You'll be able to keep your badge a little longer that way, Officer." The detective walked between the old wooden doors of the dilapidated mansion and into the building where he was greeted by a tall thin woman in tears and a mauve business suit who began to talk non-stop.

"Detective, I'm so glad you got here," the secretary said. "I was in my office working at the computer and Father Theophane had a one p.m. appointment. A young man was waiting in the parlor—I think he might have been interested in becoming a priest, and it was now one fifteen and Father Theophane had not yet appeared. He's always on time; he never goes anywhere without telling me. I began to get concerned. I buzzed his room—no answer. I buzzed Father Andrew's room and he answered. I asked if he would check on Father Theophane for me. He obliged. The next thing I knew he was yelling down the steps to call the police and also to call for an ambulance. I dialed 911 and ran up the stairs where I'm really not supposed to go, to be of service. He told me not to go in Father Theophane's room, that something horrible had happened. I asked him what. He didn't want to tell me. I pleaded with him. Finally, he said it looks as if Father Theophane is dead. Dead, I said, how could he be dead, I was with him only and hour or two before?"

As the excited lady continued to talk, a police officer was trying to get her away from the detective, but Dave waved his hand as if to say that it would be okay The secretary continued: "It turns out that Father drowned in his bathtub. I don't understand it. How can one drown in the bathtub? He must have slipped. I don't know what happened. All I know is it's horrible, just horrible."

"Where's the young man who was waiting for Father Theophane now?"

"Well, in the parlor I suppose, where I put him before all this happened."

"Please show me to the parlor, Ms...."

"*Miss* Von Kiel, if you please. Right this way Detective."

We echoed as we walked down the hall of the first floor of the mansion and eventually Miss Von Kiel opened a door. There was no sign of anyone in the room. "That's strange. I wonder when he left," she said, with a confused look on her proper and dazed face.

"Thank you ma'am." Dave went up the steps and was greeted by the coroner who took him into the bathroom where he saw a man's body face down in a bathtub brimming full with water."

"Why is his head under water? Shouldn't he be floating or something?" The coroner responded in a jaded tone: "You wouldn't float either if you had a rock tied around your neck." With that Dave ran down the steps, looking for the secretary. "Where is she, where is Von Kiel?"

"In her office," said a police officer with a gut that probably wouldn't pass inspection.

"Point me toward it."

"Right over there."

The detective turned around and flew into her office. "Don't touch your computer!"

"I was just about to, Officer. The screen saver is on, making these beautiful colored designs and I've been staring at it for a few minutes, just trying to refresh my mind, sort of hypnotized."

"Can you get rid of that screen saver without disturbing what is underneath it, that is what will then appear under it?"

"Certainly I can. I just touch the escape key and whatever was on the screen will be there again. Why do you ask?"

"Humor me, for now, Ms. Von Kiel."

"No, no, Detective, it's Miss."

"Oh yes, Ms. Von Kiel, and just touch the escape key."

With that the swirling pastels of the screen saver dissolved and a sentence appeared on the screen. "It would be better for anyone who leads astray one of these little ones who believe in me to be drowned by a millstone around one's neck in the depth of the sea."

"Did you type that on there, Ms Von Kiel?"

"No, Detective, I don't know how it got there."

"Do me a favor, please, and print that screen for me on paper."

"Certainly." She pressed the print screen key and what was on the screen came out of a printer on a sheet of paper within a few seconds and a hum.

"Thank you ma'am, very much. Please don't touch anything else. This computer needs to be dusted for fingerprints."

"Very well, Detective."

Dave went back upstairs, looked around, told the coroner he could remove the body, and supervised the collection of evidence for the next few hours. Back home, he was sitting and staring and massaging his neck without being conscious of doing any of it when the phone rang.

"I'm down the street," said a voice as pretty as the person who owned it.

"Chantal, it's good to hear you, but I don't think you'd want to be with me in my shape."

"Oh, I like your shape just fine, Dave. Sort of like an eggplant. Besides, I wanted to get even with you for that pizza bribe last night. I have Chinese food in the car and I happen to know you like Chinese."

"Now how did you find that out?" A little life was dawning.

"My friend Francis told me."

"Our friend. How did he find that out, Chantal? Probably something about those vibes he picks up."

"Let me in." Before long, Chantal was massaging Dave's neck and the man with temporary burnout was opening the food containers and sliding chopsticks out of their red paper wrappers.

"I don't know how you can use those sticks," he said. "Give me good old American silverware.

"I love using chopsticks," Chantal insisted. It really makes it feel like I'm in the Orient. And besides, I eat more slowly and less which is certainly something I need to do, especially after last night. When the lower part of my right hand gets numb I know that I'm using them correctly—only the top stick is supposed to move so, you know."

"Where did you learn, Chantal?"

"Believe it or not, Dave, Francis taught me." When we were interns, we would go to oriental restaurants once in a while. We had no time to ourselves and practically no money so once in a blue moon we would splurge." Francis always loved oriental philosophy and spirituality and he really seemed to come alive in atmospheres like that.

"By the way, Chantal," Dave stammered making an awkward transition, "sorry I got mad this morning. I guess this case is getting to me. It's been about a month and I think they're going to pull me off of it if something doesn't break soon, especially with the latest murder they gave me."

"Can you talk about it, Dave?"

"Yeah, it's a priest from that traditional Catholic group that lives in the old mansion on the other side of town. He was found in a bathtub full of water with a rock tied around his neck." Chantal dropped her chopsticks.

"You've got to be kidding!"

"No, I wish I were, Chantal."

"Dave, they're not going to pull you off of that case. There's certainly a connection there between these two deaths. They're going to want it investigated, aren't they?"

"I suppose so; I'm not thinking real clearly at this point. You see, it might be just a copycat murder."

"Or there might be a religious fanatic out there, Dave, who's also a sociopath. You know, we used to call them psychopaths. A person who appears to have no conscience, no concept of right or wrong."

"Sounds charming, Chantal. Aren't sociopaths pretty manipulative?"

"Very much so, Dave, but your first word completes the concept. They are often very charming indeed—and intelligent. They can charm a trained and experienced prison chaplain, for example, to help them get paroled only to kill him or her later when the person is no longer of use to them."

"Like I say, Chantal, charming."

"Other than that, how was your day?" she said, trying to lighten the atmosphere.

"If you want to know the truth, this is the best part of it."

"What, the Chinese food?"

"No, the delivery person."

"Dave, do you think we might be beginning to fall in love or in lust or in something?"

"I think until these cases are solved, it's 'in something.'"

CHAPTER 12

"So tell me Father Andrew, what was Father Theophane like?"

"He was a fine man," Andrew said. "He held strongly to the traditional values of the Church. He insisted on Latin in the Liturgy and wanted no part of inclusive language, or women priests, or Masses which allow lay people to be ministers in various capacities such as distributing Holy Communion, or proclaiming the Word of God during Mass. He was encouraging young people to follow in his footsteps and had several of them taught in a traditionalist seminary we have out west."

"Is your operation, excuse me, your Center, approved by the Roman Catholic Diocese?"

"Oh certainly not, we wouldn't want that. Our approval comes from God and we have a headquarters out in the west on the grounds of the seminary where we are incorporated."

Abruptly David asked: "Would Father Theophane ever consider taking his own life, Father Andrew?"

"Never; that's a mortal sin. There's no way he would ever do that."

"Forgive me for saying this, Father, but doesn't Catholic theology say that, while suicide is a grave offense, a mortal sin, that the mental capacity of some people would lessen the guilt or culpability, as somebody recently termed it for me?"

"Well, that is said, but there's so much skirting the law and so much situation ethics these days that we really don't rely on that type of attitude. Right is right and wrong is wrong and Father Theophane would never have committed suicide."

"Do you know if he had any enemies?"

"Father Theophane?—he was liked by many, many people, but because of his strongly conservative views on Church matters, his prophetic views if you will, he was also hated by some."

"Who might some of those people be, Father?"

"The radicals, you know, people who are trying to throw everything out and subvert two thousand years of tradition in the name of Vatican Council II."

"People who might read and think along the lines of Beth Johnson-Angelo?"

"Please," the priest shuttered, "don't say that name in this house. It's demonic. Yes, some of her followers are the type who would hate Father Theophane—and me for that matter. I must honestly add that Professor Johnson-Angelo would probably not countenance that sort of thing. I forced myself to read some of her writings and hate to admit it but I think she was somewhat sincere," he added with a scowl.

"Father Andrew, I'd like to track down the young man who was here for an appointment on the day that Father Theophane was murdered. Can you give me his name and address please?"

"I'm sorry, Detective, that's confidential information under the Seal of the Church."

"Father Andrew, there is no Seal of the Church in this operation. You just told me that. Now you please give me that name and address and phone number, or we'll get a search warrant and go through the entire place from top to bottom."

"I guess I have no choice. You can talk with Miss Von Kiel. Is there anything else?"

"Not for now Father. Thank you for your cooperation."

The priest left abruptly. Dave followed a few steps behind and stopped at Miss Von Kiel's door. She was busily typing at the computer. He requested the information needed and she hesitated at first but when she was told that Father Andrew approved it, she gave the detective Father Theophane's entire appointment book.

Dave drove over to the Wilson home, just a few miles away, and asked to speak with Mark. The mother of the family didn't seem all that interested when she answered the door to the modest house on a Norman Rockwell type of street. She said he's probably at the parish church where he always is. I drove a few blocks further and found a young man with closely cropped blond hair kneeling before a statue of the Blessed Mother.

"Excuse me Mark," Dave whispered, and the young man jumped up and spun around. "I didn't mean to disturb you or startle you, but I need to talk with you about Father Theophane."

"Father Theophane, I don't know any Father Theophane. Who are you?"

"I'm Detective Gold and Father Theophane used to be at the Center for Traditional Catholicism."

"Oh yeah, I know who you mean. He stood me up the other day."

"What do you mean, he stood you up, Mark?"

"Well, I had a one o'clock appointment and he never showed up for it, so I left."

"When did you leave?"

"Oh about one ten, one fifteen, something like that, Detective. Why, is something wrong?"

"Didn't you see the morning papers, Mark?"

"No, I didn't, Detective, I'm trying to keep myself away from worldly things like the newspaper."

"I see," responded the detective pensively. "Father Theophane is dead." The boy looked shocked but not shocked enough. "Have we met somewhere before, Mark?"

"No, I certainly would remember it. I don't talk to detectives very often."

"What were you at the Center for anyway?"

"Well, Detective, if you must know, I think God's calling me. In fact, I hear him all the time. He tells me I should be a priest, and he tells me I should restore the Church to its original beauty. He tells me that I should do all I can to squelch out this progressive element that has practically destroyed the Church and I wanted to tell Father Theophane that. I've been writing to him and he said to come and see him, that maybe he could get me in the seminary, but I think it was a trick. I think maybe he's a progressive that infiltrated that group and when he figured out my thoughts somehow, that he didn't show up, and God knows what would have happened to me if I didn't put all that together and get out of there quickly."

"Wow, Mark, how long has all this been going on inside of you?"

"Oh, for a long time, months, maybe longer," he said with a strange type of satisfaction.

"Have you tried to sort it out with anybody, talked with somebody?"

"Well, Detective, that's why I was going to Father Theophane but he turned on me. I was seeing a psychiatric social worker for a while but she did the same thing. Sooner or later, pretty much everybody does turn on you, you know."

"Ah yeah, maybe you're—maybe you're on to something there, I don't know."

"I sure am, Detective. Your turn will come too, you know. You'll turn on me. The only one who won't is God and maybe the Blessed Mother. That's why I'm here. Good day."

With that the young man turned around on his heal and knelt down in front of the statue of the mother of Jesus and the detective uncharacteristically stood there with his mouth open for a few moments before he left the church.

Chapter 13

Two somber looking men in black suits placed the lid on the coffin in the center aisle of the All Saints Episcopal Church. The Center for Traditional Catholicism had been granted the use of the church for purposes of the funeral as well as for other large ceremonies at times. The Requiem Mass, complete with black vestments and Latin chant, was beginning. Gold felt the Abbot tighten as the service began. Chantal looked on with the mind set of a social psychologist. Eventually, the detective whispered to Francis: "I thought you guys wore white for funerals these days."

"We do," said Francis. "They don't. Part of the mentality of the traditional Catholic movement is to keep what occurred between the fifteen hundreds and the mid-sixties when the liturgical changes began. Some of them think they're keeping what is integral to the Church. If they would go back before fifteen hundred, they would find a lot of things that were quite different from the experience they grew up with. I think there's enough room in the world and in the Church for all of this but we can talk about that at another time."

A lady with a large hat turned around and gave us a disapproving look. Well, well, look who's here, thought Gold. Our boy who lost his

vocation to the priesthood because the priest was late for his appointment is sitting a few seats up and to the left. Father Andrew gave the ser-
mon, assuring us all that the murderer would be punished, that God
was just, and the murderer would get his. On the way out of the church,
Miss Von Kiel went by, dabbing her eyes. The detective touched her arm
and expressed his sympathy. She said she was grateful. She also said she
knows it was wrong but that she was in love with the deceased priest.
Nobody knew it but her and God—not even Father Theophane. A man
of about thirty who had once been on retreat at the Salesian Monastery
greeted Abbot Francis and the Abbot answered his unspoken question.

"Yes this is not my style of Church but we're all God's sons and
daughters and here I am to celebrate that. What about you?"

"I guess I'm still searching, Abbot Francis. May I come back and
spend some more time at your monastery?"

"You certainly can. Just let us know when."

Chantal caught up with the two men as they walked toward the car.
"Wow, that incense makes me sneeze, but it sure takes me back to my
Catholic school days."

"I bet you were a knockout in that plaid jumper," Francis laughed.

"Yes I was and I spent years in therapy getting over it," she retorted.
"Actually," Chantal said, "I have a lot of fond memories of my Catholic
school days. They taught me to be strong and stand up for what I
believe in, and I really liked the nuns. Some people tell horror stories
and call themselves "recovering Catholics" but my experience was good.
I have a sense that there was just as much harshness with some of the
teachers in public schools as with some of the nuns. It's just part of life."

"We had a Rabbi in Hebrew school," announced David, "who scared
me to death. When he talked about the netherworld, I wanted to go
there then just to get away from him!"

Francis synthesized the feeling of the little group by reflexively offer-
ing a summary statement much like he would in group therapy. "I guess
we're all pretty lucky that religion didn't get in the way of our believing
in God or at least wondering about that possibility." Chantal opened her
mouth to speak but thought better of it.

CHAPTER 14

The secretary was a blend of competence, warmth, and intelligence. She knew that she was in charge and so did you. Despite her tender years, about thirty-five, she ran that office well. She put down the phone and said: "The Bishop will see you now, Abbot Francis."

"Thank you very much." Francis stood up and moved toward the Bishop's door. The door opened and the tall, thin shepherd of the diocese greeted Francis warmly.

"Please, please come in. I love to have monks in my office. It makes me feel close to God."

"Thank you, Bishop. Being called to your office makes me feel close to something as well; I'm not quite sure what it is yet." They sat on couch and chair with a little coffee table in front of them, not too far from the Bishop's large and highly polished wooden desk.

"You and I have always had a good rapport," the Bishop went on. I welcomed you to this diocese in 1987 when you were considering leaving your original order, and then encouraged your major superiors to give you a three-year leave—what do you people in monastic life call it again?

"Exclaustration, Bishop."

"That's it—permission to live out of your original cloister for another purpose. After those three years, the Holy See granted you an Indult of Departure from your original order so that you could remain in your newly founded monastery as a Salesian monk and it's been a warm and happy relationship for both of us. Is that not so?"

"That's right, Bishop. It has been and I hope it will continue."

"So do I, Abbot Francis, so do I. But you are in the middle of two murders and people are talking. It's on the front pages of the newspaper; it's on the radio and the television.

Now, I know some new religious communities in the Church opt to go the non-canonical way, that is, to live their life as best they can without seeking Church approval. Some live very much in accord with the Church and others stray from our teachings in one way or another. You have opted to remain a canonical entity and even belong to a Fellowship of Emerging Religious Communities consisting of religious from both America and Canada. I believe that there are about seven hundred groups which are in the beginning stages as new religious orders, communities, monasteries, whatever you want to call them in North America alone. You are like a tender shoot, a new plant, and you need support."

"That's true, your Excellency. You sum up our situation beautifully and you and the diocese have been kind enough to give the support you mentioned to me over the years."

"I trust your spiritual aspirations and your pastoral and professional integrity but just want to warn you that if this thing goes too far, I may have to rescind diocesan approbation because of the possibility of scandal. We don't want to be thrown into the sea with a millstone around our necks, now do we? I don't want to rescind your approbation and will try my hardest not to, but you need to know where I stand."

"That's not good news to hear, Bishop, but I respect the fact that you have been kind and honest enough to tell me this."

"Francis, that traditional Catholic group is a hot spot in the diocese. They are not under my jurisdiction but a lot of disgruntled Catholics are going there and the theologian who was murdered is also another focal point of a lot of heat, and you are involved with both of them. I must admit I've never been able to figure you out. Sometimes you appear to be living out the tradition of centuries of monastic spirituality, and at other times you seem to be forging ahead far beyond where we are."

"Bishop, I'm really not trying to do either. I look to the life of Christ for guidance and this is what seems to occur. Forgive me if I've caused you any trouble. You have enough issues to deal with these days, what with the shortage of clergy, and scandals, and money problems, and above all trying to be a spiritual presence for the People of God."

"Thank you for understanding that, Brother, it helps. Please don't take our meeting as a reprimand. To be completely honest, I admire your openness to journey with these people and try to find the truth. Most of us, probably even me, would run in the other direction. Now is there anything else I can do for you?"

"Yes, Bishop, you can give me a million dollars and some additional land, a few cars, and the time to pray, which is why I founded the monastery in the first place."

"Very well, the Bishop chuckled, mention it to my secretary on the way out. She's a real ball of fire and I'm sure she'll make it happen. Now, let's do lunch in our dining room."

CHAPTER 15

The faint smell of candle wax and new wood, and the energy of the music from the keyboard which accompanied the Night Office all hung gently in the air. Instead of leaving the oratory and going over to the hermitage where his cell was, the abbot knelt down and pulled out a small wooden prayer bench from underneath the chair behind the podium from which he sang God's praises day and night with the community. He placed the low and slightly slanted bench over his ankles. He then sat back on it and adjusted himself a bit to become more comfortable. There was but a breath of daylight left in the sky and the moon was rising, as if attracted by a huge magnet far above. The four choir stalls along the left side of the barn, along with the four along the right were outlined by the light. An uneven but soothing candle flicker from the clear sanctuary lamp hanging front right and signifying God's presence in both Word and Eucharist hinted at the open scriptures on the left and the small wooden tabernacle containing the Eucharistic bread on the right. The four foot square wooden altar stood like a dining room table, inviting, full of memories, but presently not in use.

Francis felt himself praying a mantra over and over again: "Take Lord, receive, take Lord, receive, take Lord, receive." The influence of the *Spiritual Exercises of St. Ignatius Loyola*, founder of the Jesuits, had not only permeated the spirit of his founders, St. Francis de Sales and St. Jane de Chantal, but had also seared his soul as well. Take Lord, receive from the heart of Christ to the pen of Ignatius to the soul of Abbot Francis.

Periodically, he would offer one or another of the community members up to the Lord: Sister Scholastica, Brother Matthew, Sister Jane de Chantal, Brother Benedict, the men and women Associate Members who lived in their own homes. Somewhere within him, as if a strange counterpoint, Beth Johnson-Angelo was also offered up, and then Father Theophane. Francis had a sense of being grounded. The energy of love was pouring into him and over him and through him and the negativity of recent days was being sucked out through his feet and hands. Energy moved up the base of his spine, rising to the crown of his head. Time no longer existed. Like the dawning of the day, he began to sense flame, the color orange in his spirit. After some time, he oriented himself back to the present and to the oratory and wondered about the moon. It was long gone, shining down on the oratory but not to be seen from within. He gently rose and put his prayer bench back under the chair behind the wooden podium of his choir stall and moved toward the door with complete assurance that someone was sitting on the floor in the choir stall across from his on the other side of the oratory.

CHAPTER 16

The monastery library was a bit too small for the group but it afforded more privacy than the police administration building. "All right, people," Detective Gold barked, "the only reason my boss has allowed this gathering is because of your training and ethical backgrounds, so you are required to keep this material confidential and consider yourself consultants to the police department. Agreed?"

"Agreed."

The department thanks you for your time and wants your input on the type of killer we are looking for, if indeed there is any killer to be found.

"You're using the singular," Chantal noted in her forensic psychologist voice. "Do you think it's the same person in both murders or is it still possible one was a copycat killing?"

"Here comes some of the confidential stuff," Gold responded, "and this is known only by the pathologists, myself, and the computer person who entered the data into our system. The exact same type of rope and same type of knots in the rope were found in both cases. So it was the same person who did the job in both cases as far as I can see."

Father Andrew offered his insight by saying that one person could have murdered them both or one person could have murdered one of them and then killed him—." The cleric broke off the statement midstream when he realized what he was saying.

"That's right, Father. Father Theophane could have murdered Dr. Beth Johnson-Angelo and then killed himself in the same way to make some type of statement which presently eludes me." Father Andrew stated quite categorically that this was out of the question.

"You're rather quiet Abbot Francis," Chantal observed. "Is everything okay?"

"Oh yes, I'm fine, it's just that it doesn't add up. Why would both types of people be killed if we go on the hypothesis that it was one murderer. He or she would probably have some type of hurt or anger toward the liberal end of the religious spectrum or toward the conservative end of the religious spectrum, but I don't think it would be toward both ends."

"If this person did have some feelings about religion from either angle," Gold asked, "what type of person ought we to be looking for, I mean, can you give us some sense of what the person would be like?"

"Yes, Detective, this person would probably have a great inner chasm between the religious world and the world in which he or she functions. In other words, well, it's perhaps like organized crime. The women were always to be in the church praying or taking care of the family and working hard, and the men were out 'doing business.' The men needed all of that in their lives but the religious was never really integrated, never really something which influenced their behavior—that was for the women. They had to exist side by side. For this person to have strong feelings about religion and yet break one of religion's most ancient tenants—thou shalt not kill—he or she has to have a big split within."

"Francis," Chantal asked, "wasn't your doctoral dissertation in that area?"

"Yes, yes it was, a part of it had to do with the nature of prejudice in relationship to religious values. What researchers long before me found was that there exists a good bit of prejudice throughout the religious denominations in general and it tends to be at the extreme end of the letter of the law group, called extrinsic religious orientation, and as you move over along a continuum to the spirit of the law, known as intrinsic religious orientation, you find that group to be very free of prejudice. Most of us land somewhere along this continuum but closer to the center. The prejudice appears to exist not only toward other races but toward other religions, other mind sets, other values."

"And one fascinating bit of empirical data emerged—the most highly prejudiced group of people were those who are called the indiscriminately pro-religious. That is, anything that has to do with religion of any sort, they're all for it. They don't think it through at all. They just go blindly into, yes, that's what I want. My research looked at how religious orientation affects the psychotherapeutic relationship, but I won't bore you with that. I can't resist saying this much; religious values can have a positive or negative effect upon the process and outcome of psychotherapy depending on which end of the continuum both the patient and the doctor fall."

Chantal was fascinated. "Something like the need to balance and integrate the yin and yang, female and male, light and dark within us?"

Before Francis could respond, Father Andrew, who didn't seem too happy with Abbot Francis' scholarly sharing said: "In other words, Abbot Francis, my kind of person is more prejudiced than your kind of person."

"Not necessarily, Father Andrew. It depends how far to the left or right of middle we fall. If you think of the two extremes as the ends of a straight line and then curve the line to form a circle, you notice that the two extremes meet and, I believe, share some qualities." Andrew didn't seem too comforted with the response but seemed to be pondering the metaphor in order to decide if he was insulted or not, and quieted down for the moment.

Chantal, once again the peacemaker and synthesizer, stated: "So we are probably looking for a person who is one hundred percent behind religion of any sort but sees his or her own race, religion, customs, lifestyle, etc., as the 'right' one."

"So far, so good, Chantal," Francis stated, "although we are blending two distinct research finds into one person, yet that is the nature of both applied psychology, both clinical and forensic."

"And we're looking for a person who, when around churchy sorts of things, will get right into it but when he or she sheds that role, will do whatever it takes to get by or have fun or exist in the 'secular' world. Sell raffle tickets, go to a novena or a prayer meeting, but cheat or lie without much pause because it's a 'real world' out there."

"Right again, Chantal, Francis said. It makes me cringe to hear you talk about a dichotomy between secular and sacred, Church and the real world, but that is how this sort of person would think. The indiscriminately pro-religious person wouldn't care whether Beth or Father Theophane were liberal or conservative. The extremely letter of the law or extrinsically oriented person would have more difficulty with the extremely spirit of the law or intrinsically oriented person than the other way around, in my clinical and pastoral experience.

Father Andrew asked the detective if there was any more information to which the group could be privy. Gold stated that a similar biblical quote was found on the computer at the Center for Traditional Catholicism as was found on Professor Johnson-Angelo's computer.

"Similar but not exactly the same?" asked Chantal.

"That's right, Doctor. You're sharp. Here's a copy of each. I don't know if the slight differences mean anything or not. I kind of doubt it."

Francis thought out loud and said: "If that quote were so important to the killer, he or she would have it emblazoned in the mind and be able to put it on both computers with the exact same wording and with ease. Something's funny here." As soon as the Abbot's eye hit the papers he saw something that the detective and his psychological colleague did not see. It was all over his face.

He called Father Andrew over to take a look and it was obvious that the traditional cleric saw something as well, and his face registered negativity.

"What are you two guys reacting to?" Gold said with a bit of impatience.

"The quote found on Beth's computer is the traditional wording from the Bible. It uses the pronoun 'he.'"

"Yes," joined in Father Andrew, "and the quote found on our computer is written in that repulsive inclusive language. There is no mention of he or she in the quote from our center. They use a pronoun such as 'one,' or sometimes will say he/she, but here we have 'one.'"

"So?" Gold said, his impatience mounting.

"It looks to me," offered Francis, "as if a traditional person killed Beth and a liberal person killed Andrew, yet that contradicts the fact that the same type of rope and same knots were found at both scenes.

"Could the murderer have changed his or her, I'm trying to understand this by practicing some inclusive language here, religious orientation, I think that's what you call it, between murders?"

Chantal submitted that this was very unlikely given how deeply ingrained such an orientation is and how one evolves out of a more extrinsic, structured and rigid experience of religion which is needed as a child, to a more internalized and freer experience later on. She didn't win any points with Andrew on stating that.

Francis, ever the astute clinician, summed up the discussion on the psychology of religion by noting that the latest *Diagnostic and Statistical Manual of Mental Disorders*, typically referred to as the DSM IV at long last now includes a diagnosis for people dealing with psychological issues related to religion. He read from the DSM IV:

Diagnostic code V62.89 Religious or Spiritual Problem.

This category can be used when the focus of clinical attention is a religious or spiritual problem. Examples include distressing experiences that involve loss or questioning of faith, problems associated with conversion to a new faith, or questioning of spiritual values that may not necessarily be related to an organized church or religious institution.

Gold seemed to need time to ponder all of this and digest it a little more slowly. "The information is helpful, my esteemed colleagues, but I can't see a person's religious orientation. I can only see things like murder weapons and weight and height, you know, normal human measurable stuff. Let's call it a day, folks."

"You sound like a behavioral psychologist, Dave. Moreover, you sound like many health insurance carriers, and, if you'll pardon the phrase, Chantal, you sound like the managed care companies who bury us in paperwork. Even though the Religious or Spiritual Problem diagnosis is now in the DSM IV, they still won't pay for treatment because it is in a part of the book labeled "Other Conditions That May Be a Focus of Clinical Attention." They don't see the diagnosis as a psychological illness.

Dave and Chantal dropped Father Andrew off at the Center and continued on to an East Indian restaurant. "You know, Chantal, I've been picking up some intuitive diagnostic information myself these days. Isn't that what the Abbot calls it?"

"Yes, I think it is. You sound a little sarcastic."

"Sorry, I don't mean to be, but maybe I'm a little jealous."

"Jealous, Dave, what in the world would you be jealous of?"

"When you two are around each other, there's a chemistry there. It's the only way I can put it. There's something between the two of you and I wish it were between us."

"I'm flattered, Dave, and I genuinely like you, and maybe when all this intrigue is over, there might be something more than genuine like there, but Francis and I have our acts together. As you know, we went to graduate school together and interned together, and it was during those years that he began to find himself. He realized that in his original monastery, which was large and had a lot of what they used to call daughter houses, I think they call them dependent priories now, he lived with many other monks, most of whom were priests. He always felt called to what he considered the purest form of monastic life—that is to be totally a monk and not a priest and he really saw a lot of them as clerics busy running schools, and parishes, and doing very fine work, even going off to the missions, but that a number of them were essentially diocesan priests wearing religious habits, and he felt drawn to something else."

"We put in late hours and long hours in those days, especially during internship. We worked with every sort of problem imaginable—life, death, sex, disease—these were everyday issues for us. We bonded. Francis was committed to God and monastic life. That was clear to him and to me. I loved him and he loved me and we still do love each other but he could never have a wife. He's too deceptively simple, simply complicated; I don't know what the right words are. I know that and I feel the same in my own way; most of the time it's fine."

"I am a career woman. I am very focused on my practice and I am just beginning to have a little bit of emotional and clock time available for me even to think about another serious relationship. I had a few in college that weren't all that great."

"Come on, Chantal, the vibes I feel are pretty strong between you two."

"That's true, Dave, they are, but I think that's because both of us have had a good dose of therapy in our training and we're comfortable with our bodies, with our emotions, and we know where we stand with each other. It works for us, Dave. We don't see each other for months on end and yet somehow we're soulmates."

"Weren't some of the saints like that?" Dave said, looking kind of mystified.

"Actually they were, Dave. Francis de Sales and Jane de Chantal loved each other profoundly but they also loved God passionately and it somehow created a powerful energy that spawned an entire spiritual family and here Francis is founding yet another little piece of the family in the monastery he started in 1987."

Gold scratched his head. "Seems to me you'd sort of explode with all that energy going around in you and no place for it to go."

"I think you do, Dave, but the explosion is positive. It brings more light than heat and that's the kind of light that Francis experiences sometimes with his patients."

"Oh yeah," Dave said, "like that diagnostic stuff he was talking about."

"Right, like that, Dave."

"So you two don't have anything going, right?"

"Well, Dave, we do, but it's not the kind of 'thing' that would make the news or *People Magazine*. It's something spiritual, and yes, certainly has emotional and sensual overtones, but we manage very well. Thank you very much."

"Well, if his energy goes into his prayer and ministry, where does yours go?"

"It has been going into my practice and it's just starting to seep into relationships, and I'll make myself a little vulnerable by admitting, like this one."

"Wow, you mean you're beginning to feel something for me?"

"Sure, I told you that, Dave. I just need to get all these murders out of my life, and thought that maybe you needed to get your ex-wife out of yours."

"Guilty as charged. When we first met I just had the old wounds ripped open again. She applied for a Church annulment and I got a certified letter to that effect the day Beth died."

"I'm sorry, Dave, but I know from professional experience that sometimes the annulment process can be healing; it can help a person process the failed marriage and kind of tie up some spiritual and emotional loose ends."

"Well to my mind the divorce put it behind us, but my ex has extremely strong feelings about religion and I guess wanted to go by the book on this one."

Dave's eyes widened like two pieces of root beer candy in a snowstorm as he realized what he was saying. "Don't even think it, Chantal. She would never do what you're suspecting. She couldn't."

"Why not, Dave?"

"She's severely ill and in a nursing home. That's why she divorced me—for my own good is how she put it."

"I'm so sorry, Dave, I truly am."

"Yeah, me too. Well, let's get back to those good vibes we were talking about and all that psychic and sexual energy before our food gets cold."

"I have a feeling that our vibes will keep it plenty hot, Dave!"

CHAPTER 17

"Let's walk on the road, Brother Matthew. Why sit in my office on such a glorious day?"

"Sounds good to me Abbot Francis."

"Have you been writing down the nightmares you've had in the past, along with any new ones?"

"When you asked me to do that I thought I didn't need to because I remembered them so vividly but I began writing them down because you asked me to and I realized that there's much more to them than I can remember and that much of the material would simply fade away if I didn't capture them with paper and pen.

"Exactly so, Matthew. You're very much in harmony with what a good Jungian analyst would say. You've got your notebook with you right there in your hand. Why don't you read one to me?"

"Sure, here goes. This one recurs over and over and over again. A young lady comes toward me; she's alluring, tempting, and I'm afraid you're going to throw me out if I continue on with this."

"Nonsense, Brother, you need to come to terms with your sexuality, especially if you're preparing to take your simple vows. You can't take vows as a person in turmoil, now can you?"

"My head is sure you're right but I don't want to jeopardize my life here at the monastery so my feelings resist sharing any further."

"You know that there is no obligation to share anything from the internal forum with me and I know that you realize that I care about you and your vocation. So lighten up, Matthew, you would jeopardize your call more by keeping all this penned up within than by dealing with it with someone. Now what does this lovely lady say or do when she visits you? My dreams should be so exciting!"

"Abbot, I'm a little shocked. But just a little, I kind of knew you were human. Anyway, not very much. She just kinda comes toward me and I try to get away from her and it turns into a bit of a struggle and I wind up," long pause, "killing her."

"How do you kill her, Matthew?" the Abbot asked unphased.

"Oh, sometimes I strangle her and sometimes I knife her, and sometimes I hit her with a rock—and then I experience the horror of what I'm doing. Sometimes it's already happened, sometimes I'm in the midst of it and I start to scream, really yell, and I just can't believe that I have that kind of hatred and poison within me."

"We all do, Matthew. We all do. It's the consequences of original sin, but we also have original innocence within us, and those two seem to be in conflict within you."

"Can you keep talking? It feels right to me but I don't really understand it with my head yet."

"Sure, Matthew, we are all a mixture of darkness and light, good and bad, weeds and wheat. Until that is integrated and lived with peacefully, we will always be in conflict. These things are meant to complement one another and often we have them fighting one another. For example, the sunrise is magnificent because of its contrast with the darkness, so too the sunset."

It sounds beautiful, Abbot, but I don't know what that has to do with this lady that's after me."

"Within each person are the qualities of the opposite sex, at least the ones that are stereotyped to belong to the opposite sex. So this young lady could be called your 'anima' and she represents that feminine component of who you are—and it's about time you make friends with her."

"Make friends with her! She's going to get me kicked out of here."

"That would hardly be the case, Matthew. To be a good monastic, one needs to be as whole as possible, one needs to face his or her defense mechanisms and lack of wholeness. We're filled with prejudices, and filters and opinions, and as we move through life we can shed a lot of them. Initially, they orient us to life, to God, and are helpful, but they can limit us as we evolve. That part of things will come a little later for you probably but for now it seems as if God is inviting you to make friends with your anima and become a bit more whole. She can give you the interior freedom to remain here and live a fruitful monastic life."

"How do I begin that process, Abbot?" the shaken novice said half-heartedly.

"You can start by talking to her."

"Talking to her? Are you serious?"

"Yes, that's right my brother. Rerun the dream in your mind and extend the ending. Make friends with her. Tell her you're sorry. Ask for forgiveness. Get to know her. Find out her name."

"That sounds harder than trying to get a date for the prom when I was in high school."

"Oh, give me a break, Matthew. A great guy like you must have had plenty of opportunities for dates."

"Well, I did, Abbot, but I guess I was a bit of a prude and I was sort of afraid that I would be tempted beyond my strength."

Do you know what alchemy is, Matthew?

"Isn't it the medieval quest to change base metals into gold?"

"Yes, Matthew, but there is a deeper and more philosophical and spiritual meaning to the quest. The Chinese have a very ancient tome called *The Secret of the Golden Flower*. Much too simply put, in it they discuss internal alchemy, or the use of meditation to light a symbolic fire below the naval to heat an imaginary cauldron above it thereby changing our generative energy into a more spiritual vapor which rises up to meet the energy of our heart and then moves up to our mind. The transformed energy begins to circulate throughout the body eventually. Modern psychologists might call this sublimation—the transformation and constructive use of one form of human energy to another. Maybe you can ask Jesus to transform some of that energy for you."

"Please try not to let your fear stop you, Matthew. Please try to do what I suggest and ask the Lord for help; the Spirit will guide you. The Spirit is energy, the Spirit is life and you're full of both. Don't be so afraid of it, my friend. I've got to get back now. I have a patient waiting."

"I suppose I have someone waiting too. Thank you—I think."

CHAPTER 18

"John, please come into the office where there's a little more space and a lot more light."

"Thank you, Abbot. I'd like to tell you that I'm feeling a good bit more comfortable now that we've had a couple sessions."

"That's good news. Please sit down and let's talk. How are you and your patients?"

"Well, my patients are healing me. It is good to be able to do what I've been trained to do and help a few lives."

"I couldn't agree with you more. Your real healing will come with the passage of time, the time you need to go through the mourning process in your own unique style. Don't let anyone hurry you or tell you that you are young and will re-marry. No one will ever replace Beth. People mean well but often retard the mourning process by such comments. And when we can get this murder solved you'll be even freer to heal. Research shows that while litigation of any sort is going on, it is difficult to get on with healing. Some studies, for example, were done on accident victims who thereby became pain management patients. They made some progress before court, but much more after the legal issues were resolved one way or another. Sorry for rambling on, my friend; I used to be a teacher."

"What you say is helpful and fascinating, Abbot, and I know that there is a method to your madness. Everything you do is calculated to help me heal and I appreciate that very much. You said murder a moment ago. Are you convinced that Beth did not commit a very bizarre type of suicide to make some kind of statement which still eludes most of us?"

"I'm working on the hypothesis that Beth's life was taken from her, John, not the other way around. I have some reason to believe that but the police won't allow me to share certain information, so let's just keep a good thought in that regard, okay?"

"I'm happy to, Abbot, but also very curious and I know that you can understand why. My respect for you, however, helps my self-discipline."

"The respect is mutual, John. And now onward. We've spent a good bit of time processing some of your thoughts and feelings and we've tried to come to terms with the 'two steps forward and one step backward' of the mourning process and how it sneaks up on you when you're feeling pretty good and clobbers you. We also discussed the fact that those moments of feeling pretty good can gradually stretch over the months from moments to hours and days and then to the rest of your life."

"I know we did and I believe you, but it seems so far away and it doesn't feel as if I'll ever get there."

"Well, John, let's take another look at it. Let's look at it through the vehicle of your body. I think it's time to calm down that restless gut of yours."

"Okay, but I'm not sure what to do or what this process is all about."

"Oh, you mean the Therapeutic Touch. Well, did you read the literature I gave you?"

"Yes, I did. It was extremely interesting. I respect the scientific studies along with the philosophical foundation on which Therapeutic Touch rests but you're not using any EEG machines or any EKG machines or stethoscopes, and I guess I still need some instruments because that's how I was trained."

"Well, let's just use the instruments provided through the energy of all life which I see as Christ and you can see in any way you like, perhaps higher power would fit you at this point. I'll use my hands to read your energy field, as it were, and to cleanse, replace, and free up your energy."

"Human hands as instruments of healing, somehow that seems more appropriate than electronic gizmos of steel and plastic. As for the higher power issue, Abbot, I was raised Catholic and I do resonate with the concept of Christ, although right now I'm in such pain I'm not sure what I believe."

"That's okay Jesus can handle confusion. In fact I believe that he had to deal with his own confusion while here on earth. Scripture tells us that he was like us in everything but sin. But enough of that."

"Now, I can do Therapeutic Touch with you simply sitting on a bench but I think you will find it a little more restful to lie down on a massage table, listen to the taped music I put on, and just kind of drift off, okay?"

"Fine by me. I feel like I am already starting to drift off, as you call it."

"There's no need to take your clothing off, especially since you are in shorts and that comfortable looking tee-shirt with the stone work and masonry ad on it."

"A gift of my cousin Vinnie."

"My tee shirts all have ads on them too—usually for a school or a professional association. At any rate, you can take off your sandals and hop up on the table, lying on your back please. Now just pray a little to yourself in any way you like. We call it centering. Just choose to be open to the energy of God, of goodness, of healing, the energy that flows through all of creation—trees, rocks, plants, animals, people, and I'm going to scan your body with my hands, that is, I'm going to move my hands slowly from the top of your head down to the soles of your feet and tune in to your energy field. There—I sense it very easily right here, an inch or two above your head. Now please turn on your side for a few moments while I scan your back."

"It is easy to pick up a lot of negativity dealing with the illnesses and problems of others and, of course, because of your wife's death. It stays with us like static cling. To rid you of the negative energy or toxins, I'll do a little back, neck, and foot massage to loosen up your field, okay?"

"My soul is in your hands, as is my body. I trust you."

"Now, on your back again. I am opening my hands like two rakes or combs and letting the negativity cling to my hands which I'll shake periodically to get rid of the poisonous energy I collect on them as I pass through your energy field. I am passing my hands through your energy field and breaking up what you are emitting as well as what I have shifted around, changed the frequency of, whatever you want to call. I'm going to massage the bottom of your feet a little more just to kind of loosen them up and I'd like you to think about negative energy that is going to flow out of your feet. Just think of the poisonous negativity leaving you primarily through the soles of your feet. I'll do a little massage of your spine and neck and I'd like you to just think of the word "flow." You can use it as a mantra or prayer word and just gently say to yourself, if you like, "flow, flow, flow" or just kind of space out and relax. Just don't get too weirded out by all of this."

"I was going to say, Francis, that I hope I'm not messing anything up by talking at this time, but you have me laughing and even with that possible distraction I'm still beginning to feel some sensations as you are doing whatever this is with me."

"We call it unruffling the field, John, and people sometimes feel intense feelings from the past during bodywork. The practitioner sometimes has to deal with transferred anger, pain, whatever as a result. But, that's okay; it comes with the territory and Jesus had the same type of thing to deal with in his own way."

"I'm understanding your theological musings pretty well, thanks to being married to a theologian. Also, Francis, as you unruffle my field, I'm beginning to feel—it's hard to describe—a sensation of cleansing, a sensation of almost electrical changes in my body."

"I understand what you're saying, John. People experience and conceptualize this in different ways. Stay with me and just allow the junk to flow out of you. Remember that it's leaving through your feet as well. I've just moved my hands down—now over your chest and stomach and now over your hips and your legs and your feet. If you roll on your side again I'll do the same thing down your back. I'll unruffle the field there as well, cleansing you from the negative energy you've picked up. That's right."

"As you move downward, Francis, I feel it even more intensely, especially down my back and specifically along my spine and around my kidneys."

"That's fine, John. Remember that people experience this in a variety of ways. Just have your own experience of it and I'll move all the way down to your feet, and while you're in this position I'll return to you head and put some energy into you now. Once again, try to remember that we are all part of a huge energy pool and that I think of the energy of Christ, I think of grace. You think of this energy in whatever way is comfortable for you and I'll more slowly now move my hands gently through your energy field with the intention of letting God's energy pass through me and into you, not my energy, it's energy from someone else. I'm just an energy conduit. That's right, just be with the process. I think something just happened there, John."

"I think something happened there too, Francis. In fact, I know that it did. It happened to us both at the same time. I sensed a deeper connection, or you kind of poking through my field somehow right around my kidneys."

"John, as you know, above the kidneys are the adrenal glands and they are sometimes very sensitive to a need for more energy and I'm just going to stay there for a little while and let the adrenals suck up this energy. I can feel a type of a drawing or pulling through my hands and we'll just take a little time and you can listen to the music I have playing in the background as you drift of and internally strengthen and grow."

A few minutes passed and Francis moved his hovering hands on down through the body to the feet once again and had John turn on his back and experienced himself becoming intensely focused on John's eyes.

"John, I'm putting the palms of my hands lightly over your eyes and my intention is to give you some energy but I'm also going to move my hands around in a kind of waving motion over your eyes to allow energy to flow. There's a block there. It feels like there's a void right around your eyes. I'm going to move that and yet I get the feeling that this is the only part of things that you're not comfortable with."

"That's right, Francis, I'm not and I can't seem to explain why—to you or to myself. Just before you moved your hands to my eyes, perhaps when you began to feel drawn to them, I became filled with terror for a moment. Much of it has passed, but I'm still feeling up tight."

"I have some idea as to what is happening, John. I think there's something in your life which you don't want to see."

"Do you have any idea at all what it is, Francis?"

"Not yet, John, but it's something very traumatic and it's probably not something in the present tense. I might also mention that my intuitions are often one to two days behind my encounter with a patient and come when I am least expecting them. At any rate, you seem blinded to something out of fear."

"What in the world do you mean by that, Francis. I'm really trying hard to follow you here but it's getting more and more challenging."

"Just let go of rigid logic for a little while, John, and enter into a deeper kind of logic. In clinical hypnosis we call it trance logic. I have an intuitive sense that there's something you have seen that you don't want to recall so you're blinding your mind's eye to it. Do you follow that?"

"Yes, I do, Francis. It makes me a little uncomfortable and I don't like to admit it, but I do follow you."

"Well, good. Be with that. Try to absorb that insight and don't work at making it happen; just let it happen and it will. Now, you seem awfully tight in a few places. I'll just give you a little more energy and get your energy to flow a little more around your eyes, and down around your feet, and then we had better conclude for today."

"I feel frightened and confused, Francis, but I also feel encouraged and liberated."

Fright, confusion, and compassion hung in the air like the graceful branches of a willow tree not sure where they wanted to move in the breeze.

CHAPTER 19

Chantal was in her little metallic blue Sundance stuck on Route 80. Lots of visitors were in the Poconos to enjoy the fall foliage and glut the roads. She reached over and turned on the radio to distract her from the obsessional thoughts she was having about the two murders, and growing feelings about Dave.

"Yes, go ahead caller, you're on WVPO talk radio."

"I think that the lady you are interviewing is way out of line. She's trying to change everything in the Church. She's talking about the feminine qualities of God, the ordination of women, and married clergy. What next? The Bible says people like her should have a millstone hung around their necks and be drowned."

"Well, that's your opinion, caller. Thank you."

"Do you have any response to that, Professor?"

A woman's voice responded: "I wish the caller well."

"And that's a perfect way to wrap up for today. You've been listening to an interview with author and theologian, Professor Beth Johnson-Angelo. Until next time, take care."

"Chantal's right hand flew to the radio, shut it off, picked up the phone, dropped it, untangled the cord from the gear shift, picked it up again, and punched in "O" for operator.

"Operator, this is Dr. Chantal Fleur, forensic psychologist consulting with the Police Department. It is imperative that I get in touch with WVPO radio right away. I don't have the number. I'm stuck in my car on Route 80."

"Very well, Doctor, if it is an emergency I'll see if I can get the number. A minute later the operator said: "The number is…." Chantal interrupted her and asked her to dial it for her.

"As I said, I'm stranded on Route 80 and this is extremely important. It concerns a double murder investigation."

"Very well, Doctor, and thanks for using Commonwealth Telephone, and I hope you catch him."

A young man's voice trying to sound grown up answered "WVPO."

Chantal tried to remain calm and professional as she spoke: "This is Dr. Fleur working for the Police Department. I just heard a caller on your talk radio program and it's crucial that I find out more about him."

"That was a tape from over a month ago, Doctor, and there's nothing we really know about our callers other than what you hear on the air."

"Well we need to get a copy of that tape immediately and have it analyzed."

"I'm sorry, Doctor, the voice said a little uneasily. I can't do that. I'm an East Stroudsburg University student interning here. I don't know why they give me all this responsibility on a Sunday afternoon."

"Well, I'll be over with a detective before very long and we'll straighten it out and save your hide as well."

"Much appreciated, Doctor. I could have used that many times over the years."

"Police Headquarters," a woman's voice said on the phone.

"This is Doctor Fleur, a consultant for the department."

"Just a moment please." The woman was back on in about a minute and said" "Yes, I have your information right here. How can I help you, Doctor?"

"It's extremely important that I talk with Detective Gold as soon as possible."

"He's in the car right now but I'll see if I can patch you through, Doctor Fleur."

"After a few extraterrestrial noises, the Detective's voice came over the telephone."

"Chantal, what's going on?"

"I think I just heard our murderer call in on a talk show. I called WVPO in Stroudsburg to find out more and they couldn't help me."

"I'm on my way, Chantal, I'll meet you there. I'll do my best Dave, I'm stranded on Route 80 East."

Chantal crept along in her car about a tenth of a mile frustrated and anxious. About twelve minutes after she made her call a car was driving along the shoulder to the right of traffic with red and blue blinking lights. It stopped next to hers. What now, she thought with a sigh. Chantal looked over and there was Dave waving her into his car. She shut off her car, leaving it unlocked in case someone wanted to move it, and hoped for the best as she got into Dave's car. They continued along the shoulder, off the ramp, and on to the radio station which was less than a mile away. "So near yet so far," she murmured.

The couple went into the WVPO radio station and found no one in sight. They knocked on a few doors and eventually a young man in his early twenties welcomed them into a room filled with tape decks, little colored lights, and CDs.

"Dr. Fleur," he said while extending his hand, "I'm Tom. We spoke on the phone."

"Thank you for your welcome, Tom. This is Detective Gold."

"I called the station owner and he said to give you anything you want so here's a copy of the tape you were looking for. As I said, there's nothing on it but the show that you heard on your car radio and we have no way of knowing who's who when people call in."

"That fine, Tom. You are a life saver."

"Keep up the good work, my boy; you're going to go far," said Gold with a smile as they turned and left the building. In Gold's car they popped the tape into the cassette player and fast-forwarded it through a number of different voices. Chantal reminded him that it came toward the very end of the program. When Gold realized that he had finished the tape he rewound it a bit and heard the announcer asking for the last caller of the day to speak.

"That's it, she said. Gold listened, as did Chantal, and they both felt ice forming up and down their spines.

"Recognize the voice?" Gold asked.

"No, how about you, Dave?"

"No, but maybe someone else will. You're a good detective, Chantal, not bad at all as a forensic psychologist either."

Chapter 20

"The doctor will see you now," said the woman behind the reception desk to the twenty-five year old man with short blond hair and hazel eyes.

"Thank you, ma'am. I can use a doctor."

John Johnson-Angelo greeted his patient as reassuringly as he could. The young man had lost his first-born child just a few weeks ago due to a high fever. John had done everything he could. As soon as he saw the child he rushed him off to emergency but it was too late. A viral infection that could have been treated earlier was not, and the little girl died.

"How are things, Rob? I'm sure it's still a struggle."

"Yes, it is, Doctor. I've been better, that's for sure."

"And your wife?"

"Well, she's trying to be very strong but it's certainly taken a toll on her as well. Doctor, I 'm here because I'm very depressed and I don't know where else to turn. Is there some kind of pill you can give me?"

"What you're experiencing, Rob, is reactive depression—a normal response to a trauma. It's going to take a lot of time to pass through the mourning period and adjust to life without your daughter. Mourn in your own way—be quiet, be noisy, read, hike, sleep, and try to keep your life as normal as possible."

"How long will it take, Doc?"

"It's different for everyone, Rob, and each person mourns differently. Some people get quiet, some people won't stop talking about the situation, some people lose themselves in reading or work, some people eat, some people sleep. What do you do, Rob?"

"I'm not sure what I do; all I know is I feel like I want to get even with fate, God, luck, chance, whatever or whoever it was that caused this."

"Do you have a clergy-person you can talk to, Rob?"

"I think religion is extremely important but I guess you'd say I'm in a kind of transition right now. At this point I just let religion kind of be religion, and I do business as I need to do it."

"I'm not sure what you mean by all that, Rob."

"I'm not real sure what I mean by it either, Doc. Can't you just give me some medicine to take?"

"Well, there are medications and if you really want it I can give you something, but that's like putting a Band-Aid on a broken leg. Your kind of depression is not based on biology but is based on a painful life experience. I'll write out this prescription for something mild, take it as directed, try to get some exercise, and try to process this with someone. In fact I have a good friend who is a very fine clinical psychologist as well as a deeply spiritual person. Maybe you'd want to talk with him."

"Yeah, Doc, I think that might do it. That might be the way to go."

"Let me speak with him first, Rob, and see if I can set things up. He's a very busy man. And then I'll get back with you. He can also monitor your response to the medication I give you. About eighty per cent of psychotropic medications are prescribed at the advice of psychologists. They are in the front lines and are often well trained in psychopharmacology and make excellent recommendations and observations. How does all of that sit with you?"

"Perfect, Doc. You are a life saver. I hope that I'm not out of line by saying that I'm especially grateful to you because I know that you are dealing with the loss of your wife at this time. You are a very credible person to advise me about grief."

Chantal soaked in a bathtub full of bubbles and sipped a large iced tea. She had a mountain of paper work to do but knew she deserved this rest and that if she didn't take care of herself she would be no good for anyone else. Underneath the main theme of the murders in her life these days was the sub-theme of David Gold. He certainly had charisma and strength. She liked those qualities in a man. There was also a tenderness there, and once in a while a little vulnerability slipped through. Why wasn't she letting herself feel her feelings about Dave? She sat with that question for a while and the information seemed to surface, just the same way the bubbles did from the water. Francis appeared in her mind's eye. He was spoken for and she knew it. She had also clearly reconciled herself a long time ago to the platonic relationship that they enjoyed. Was this some type of regression? Maybe it had to do with the intensity of their work of late. It was like a flashback to internship days.

This life and death stuff and the various religious ceremonies associated with things was also stirring up some deep archetypal feelings of God and the Church and her spiritual life. Why did she continue to pray spontaneously and ask for guidance and help when she didn't even know if she believed? Why were so many of her friends so deeply religious, including Dave?

Across town a weary detective was staring at a TV screen and absorbing none of it. His mind was filled with Chantal. What was the resistance within him to her presence in his life all about? Was it some

excessive type of loyalty that the adult child of an alcoholic often mani-
fests? His wife was gravely ill and had divorced him. Wasn't he free yet?
What was the probability of something like that happening again?
Besides, he and Chantal are of different religions. He's Jewish and she's
agnostic, if that's a religion. He loved his Jewish roots and yet was
strangely attracted to the contemplative side of the way Francis was living. There's a whole history of mysticism in Judaism. Maybe it's about
time he took a closer look at that.

CHAPTER 21

"John, thanks for taking time out of your busy schedule to come by. I know we weren't scheduled to meet until next week," said Francis. "I'd really like to see you feeling better as soon as possible. How have you been doing with the self-hypnosis techniques I taught you last time?"

"Very well, Francis, I have been very faithful. Nurses and doctors are notoriously bad patients but I've been a good one. I've done what you asked me to ten to twelve times a day for just about a minute every hour or two, whenever I could, and I certainly feel better in my gut. My depression is lifting a bit but my eyes feel funnier than ever."

"Well, that's quite a bit of progress, John. As I mentioned last time, brief and frequent exposures to self-regulatory procedures such as clinical hypnosis, biofeedback, the Relaxation Response techniques and the like are often found to be more effective than doing them once or twice a day for say twenty minutes at a shot. By taking out a minute every hour or two you are weaving into your day a very healing experience and lowering the level of collected stress and tension and thereby keeping things from building up to where they physically or emotionally spasms."

"Your point is very well taken and I've experienced it, Francis. But what about my eyes?"

"That's why I asked you to come by, John. You have seen something and you can't look at it again."

"Is it seeing Beth dead in the water?"

"No, John, that's not my sense. I'll come right out with it. I get the sense that you've seen the killer."

John looked like a lightening bold just went through him. "How in the world could I have seen the killer?"

"I'm not sure yet. My sense is that you saw the killer and if you open up to it you will be able to recognize him."

"Recognize him? That sounds like a really tall order, Francis, and I'm sorry if I sound angry. It's more shock than anything else. How can I open myself up to this, Francis?"

"Well, John, I'll do some hypnosis with you here in the office and a little more Therapeutic Touch, but I think what will probably be most helpful is simply a little quiet meditation. One way of approaching it in both the yogic and Catholic Christian traditions is through a meditation technique Christians call Centering Prayer. You simply take a prayer word and gently say it over and over again to yourself for a while and often that prayer word slips away and your mind clears. It's thought to be a preliminary way of opening oneself up to contemplation. I see it as a way of opening oneself up to the profound energy that exists in the universe. In that energy is wisdom and courage. My thought is that you might want to spend a little time here at the monastery to do that. You can come over and sit in the oratory after your last patient in the evening for twenty minutes or a half hour. Do you think you can swing that?"

"I think so, Francis. It's not that much of a drive and I'm not doing anything else very constructive these days. Shall I start tonight?"

"Wow, you really are being a good patient. Please do. You can stop by for the Night Office at eight thirty if you want or if you don't make it in time for that just come into the oratory whenever you like. I'll probably be in there praying and, John, don't worry about anyone else who may be there or about any other sensations or presences you may feel."

"What is that supposed to mean, Francis?"

"It's not important; I just want you to be comfortable. The atmosphere is sometimes charged with a lot of energy in that oratory."

"I'm not sure if that comforts me or frightens me. Oh well, I've gone this far...."

CHAPTER 22

"I'm sure that the police have been over this with you many times, Miss Von Kiel but I've been going over and over the death of Father Theophane in my mind and I need your help."

"Certainly, Father Andrew, what can I do for you?"

"Just tell me once again what your morning was like prior to our finding Father Theophane dead."

"Well, I arrived here for work promptly at eight-thirty as usual and took several phone calls. I did some word processing on the computer, and also did a little filing. It was a pretty day so I went out back and ate my lunch from eleven-thirty to twelve-thirty during which time I also did a little reading and praying. The Center was very quiet and I knew Father Theophane had a one o'clock appointment with a young man so I made sure I was back in the house in plenty of time for the young man's arrival."

"And at what time did the young man arrive, Miss Von Kiel?"

"About twelve forty-five, Father. I put him in the parlor and expected Father Theophane to come down promptly, which he always does. When he was not down on time, I gave him about ten minutes and then rang his room. There was no answer and that's when I rang your room."

"So there was a time when someone could have very easily walked into the building and up the stairs into Father Theophane's room?"

"Yes, that's certainly true, Father. As you know Father Theophane is a very regular person. He takes a brisk walk every day between eleven and twelve. He comes back and showers, reads some Scripture, and then often has appointments from one o'clock on." Her eyes welled with tears and unspoken pain.

"I can't help thinking, Miss Von Kiel, that the murderer knew Father Theophane's schedule. I believe he slipped into his room when he was showering, hit him over the head or something like that, and then slipped a noose around his neck and stopped up the tub until it filled with water."

Flinching, she responded: "That makes a morbid kind of sense to me, Father. My only question is why."

"Frankly, Miss Von Kiel, there are people who think that they are doing right by getting rid of traditionalist Catholics. So many sins have been committed in the name of the Lord. As you know, I think that all of this liberated so-called theology is anathema but Christ is never served in violence. Thanks for your help, Miss Von Kiel."

"You're very welcome, Father."

As he walked out of the office, the priest was angry at himself for thinking that the secretary he had just spoken with so rationally had all the opportunity in the world to kill his partner at the Center. She certainly was not the type and what would motivate her to do such a thing any way?

CHAPTER 23

"Lord, open my lips," sang Francis as he traced the sign of the cross over his lips with his right thumb. The community chanted in response: "and my mouth shall declare your praise."

It was perfectly dark in the oratory, with the exception of the candle flame, as the community celebrated the liturgical Office of Vigils during which they keep watch for the Christ who breaks into their day and who will come again at the end of time. After psalm ninety-five, which is a call to worship and a dialog between Francis and the group and long ago memorized by all, some soft lighting illuminated the interior of the sacred space.

Francis tried to join the group in reciting the psalms back and forth and struggled to keep his mind on the readings from Scripture, the early fathers and mothers of the Church, and from his own founders, Saint Francis de Sales and Saint Jane de Chantal, but was intensely aware of the rising feeling within him that something was about to break lose. He had an overwhelming sense that John had been to the oratory to pray last night. John's presence still lingered in the air. Was he neglecting the community by being so involved with these murders? Would the Bishop require another "command performance" from him? He loved

Chantal's presence in his life but was he giving her or Dave or anybody else wrong ideas? The "break even" financial picture of the monastery was leaning toward pink, if not red.

Silence—a sense of everyone waiting for someone or something. Then he realized that the community was waiting for him to end the office with the usual prayer and so he did, trying not to sound startled or hurried: "Come Lord Jesus!" With that one or two sat down in their choir stalls and the others left the oratory. There were a man and a woman there on retreat and Francis had barely met them, let alone seen either of them privately for spiritual direction. He guiltily hoped that they were having a good experience. He always told retreatants that the Holy Spirit was really the retreat director. That would literally have to be the case this time around.

The abbot sat in the darkness, closed his eyes, and just let his head clear. This was supposed to be *Lectio Divina* time. This was supposed to be a time of meditation and contemplation, perhaps sparked by the prayerful reading of Scripture or the writings of the monastic fathers and mothers. Francis's contemplation this morning came straight from his heart and was largely a cry of the blind and deaf people from the Gospel for the Lord's help.

I want to do your will, my God. I think I'm doing it, but if I'm not, please let me know. In the quiet darkness he knew that something was brewing in the universe and it involved him. "Come Lord Jesus, Come Lord Jesus" echoed over and over in his mind. As if some time warp, an hour and a half had passed and the bell was ringing for Morning Prayer, the office of Lauds. The community gathered once again and the sun was now rising.

Francis gave a knock on the side of his choir stall and the group stood up as he intoned: "O God, come to my assistance," making the sign of the cross from forehead to chest and from shoulder to shoulder along with the others. The psalms were sung and a reading from Scripture was proclaimed. The canticle of Zachary was sung, reminding those assembled of redemption, resurrection, new life, and the time for the intercessions for the needs of the world at large came. Various people spontaneously offered prayers for the sick, the poor, the guests at the monastery, etc. Francis prayed out loud for the recently departed and interiorly for his own peace and openness to whatever role he would play in solving the mystery of their deaths. He chanted the final prayer and blessed the community and the work of their hands that day and all departed in silence for an informal breakfast of coffee, toast, cereal and then it was off to work for everyone.

The phone rang on Francis' desk. He picked it up and was greeted by John's voice.

"Yes, I am meditating regularly. Thank you for the use of the oratory. It really helps. I'm feeling quite refreshed and strengthened. My eyes feel more peaceful and, perhaps more importantly, I have a memory of a car parked near our house when I left to go and tend to my patients the night Beth was killed. It may be nothing but I think there could be more to it than that. All I can do is keep open, I suppose."

"That's right, John, you're doing really well," said Francis in a peaceful and encouraging tone.

"I'll be seeing you in a few days, right?"

"That's for sure, John, and maybe you'll be seeing more than me."

"In the meanwhile, I have a patient whom I'd like to refer to you if it's okay—a young man who recently lost his little infant daughter and who is very depressed and spiritually conflicted."

"Okay John; I'll do what I can. As you know, there are never enough hours in the day but if he calls me I'll do my best to see him at least one time, okay?"

"Good enough, Francis, thanks for everything. I'll be talking to you soon. I'm grateful. Bye."

Francis had put aside the hours of the morning to get some paper work done and with the exception of a couple phone calls was able to do pretty well. Shortly before eleven, he walked over to the main building and into the library where the community was assembled for Chapter. The meeting takes its name from the ancient practice of reading a chapter of the Rule before the community discusses any business it needs to attend to. After a brief prayer led by the Abbot, Sister Jane de Chantal read from the Rule: "A reading from the Holy Rule of the Salesian Monastic Community."

> The monks and nuns live the Salesian monastic life in response to the Lord's call. An integral part of each monastery is the guest house, a place through which others enjoy and share in the monastic atmosphere in order to renew themselves.
>
> Ministry, be it manual labor, professional services, pastoral care, etc., is also a part of our life. Work outside of the monastery is not to exceed the time limits of a half-time position, ideally carried out during the day. This will leave early morning and late afternoon and evening free for contemplation and community life.

"Thank you, Sister Jane. I don't have much to say this morning. I know I'm usually talking about some material needs such as a broken pipe or a paint job needing to be done or asking you to prepare for one guest or another, but this time I'll leave it completely up to you. Does anyone have anything to say for the good of us all? Things were quiet for a moment and then Francis said: "Sister Scholastica you look like you'd like to speak but are not quite sure if you want to."

"You are exactly right, Abbot Francis. Thanks for your encouragement. It's just that the reading we just read from the Holy Rule got me thinking that you work too hard. You certainly work a lot more than a half-time position. It's more like time and a half and lately it's been more of that than ever. I don't feel neglected and I don't think the others do either but I am concerned for your health and well-being."

"Thank you, Sister, I truly appreciate that. As you all know, I've been involved in two murder investigations along with my other work. When this thing clears, I promise that I will take a few hermit days, either at the ashram or over at the Jesuit Center where, as you know, I minister part-time."

Brother Benedict spoke up. "That sounds good to me, we need our founding Abbot. Keep your strength up. You're supposed to outlive me, remember?"

"Thank you, Brother, I'll leave that up to God."

The joke seemed to break the tension.

"Brother Matthew, you look like you're in good spirits today. How are things?"

"Oh, I'm doing well, Abbot Francis. I'll be talking with you about it very soon. I feel a little guilty because I think maybe I'm a part of your burden."

"No, please don't feel that way. That's why I'm here. You are a priority. I'm feeling some guilt because I've not been able to give the community the attention it deserves. The four others responded almost in unison 'That's not true.'"

Brother Benedict summed up for the community, "I'm the oldest here and I've seen a lot of monastic life. I transferred here from a very busy monastery to lead a simpler life, closer to what monasticism started out like and I'm glad that I did. We have more than we need from you and the Lord, so I think we're all saying that all is well but just to be careful not to over-extend, and to get some rest when things calm down a bit."

"Well," sighed the Abbot, "it sounds as if the voice of the Spirit is coming through loudly and clearly and I will listen to what you have to say and am grateful for it. I think each of us could stand a little recreation or maybe some quiet time, whatever you prefer. How about if anyone who wants to, goes over to the state park one day this weekend. That is sometimes fun for me but right now I would be very happy just to sit outside and maybe do some busy work to let my mind clear. All in favor?"

Everybody responded in the affirmative, and since it seemed like all were in agreement and that the meeting was ending and on a happy note. Francis, however, felt some discord in his gut.

CHAPTER 24

A young lady was mixing a batch of something in the kitchen. She was trying to be productive and get her mind off of her recent loss. Her husband dialed the phone from the living room. "This is Rob Williams calling. Would it be possible to speak to Abbot Francis?"

"This is he, Rob. How can I help you?"

"Doctor Johnson-Angelo gave me your name and number. He said you might be willing to meet with me."

"More than willing, Rob. When can you make it?"

"Well, I work days but can come any evening or weekend that's convenient for you, Abbot."

"I sense a lot of pain in your voice, Rob. Why don't you come over today?"

"That would be wonderful. I didn't want to ask. I can be over to your place any time you like."

How about early this afternoon, say about twelve-thirty?"

"Sounds good to me. See you then."

The community gathered for Midday Prayer which is the briefest of the Offices, taking about ten or twelve minutes. They dress informally for this celebration of the Liturgy since it is often sung in the fields or the laundry or the bakery, wherever monastics are working in larger monasteries. Midday Prayer is a little oasis of prayer in the day which can seem a bit annoying to a busy person but in reality is refreshing and can help to anchor one in prayer life so that the monastic does not drift too far afield from what his or her life is all about. At the end of the Office everyone bowed to the presence of the sacred as manifested in the front of the oratory by cross, altar, bible, and tabernacle, and then filed out.

The rest of the community looked like it was on its way to a beach party. They had relaxing clothes on and a cooler with some sandwiches and beverages in it and some books to read. It was their day for the state park.

"God be with each of you," said the Abbot. "I'll keep the home fires burning on this late summer day. Have a wonderful time and come back whenever you feel like it. Don't feel obliged to any time constraints. I know some of you will enjoy being off and being quiet and others of you might like to chat—whatever will be fun for you. Just enjoy."

"You have a good time too," some of the members shouted back as they hopped in the car.

"A good time working?" Brother Benedict hollered out. The gang laughed and drove off. Francis walked back to the Hermitage. He was on edge and more than a little startled to find someone sitting in his waiting room.

"Oh, you must be Rob."

"Yes, I am, Abbot, I'm sorry I'm a little early."

"That's all right, I'm just taken off guard a little bit. If you wait just a minute, I'll be right with you."

Francis walked through the waiting room and into his office where he checked his answering machine, finding that the message light was flashing. He heard Chantal's voice when he played the message.

"Give me a call when you can, Francis. I have a tape I'd like you to listen to. It could help us solve things." Francis scribbled Chantal's name on a pad of paper by the phone and erased the message.

"Please come in now, Rob," Francis said as he opened the door, "and let's see what we can do." The young man stood up awkwardly and entered the office. "Please have a seat on the couch," said the Abbot, "and I'll sit here across from you. How do you like the couch and chair? They're a matching set."

"They look fine to me," Rob said with a little confusion in his voice.

"Well, they look even more than fine to me," said the Abbot. "You see they're my favorite brand—'early yard sale.' The other couch I had was pretty difficult to get out of once you got into it. In fact I needed the jaws of life for a few people, so I looked around and one day was able to find this bargain on somebody's lawn. Well, enough about me and my furniture. I'd like to take a little clinical history if I may."

"That's fine by me, Abbot."

"Good. I don't usually write during sessions but the first time through I do some writing just to get some general background and that kind of focuses me so that I am better able to do what I can to help. I have your name, address, and phone number, etc. from Dr. Johnson-Angelo. He also told me something about the situation. I'm so very sorry about the death of your daughter."

"Thank you, Abbot. I appreciate that."

"Now then, can you tell me a little something about your medical history?"

"Not much to tell there; I don't even wear glasses."

"So, Rob, you eat okay and sleep okay and don't take any medication?"

"That's right, Abbot, and I'm happy to report it."

"Good to hear it. How about your psychological background? Have you had any psychotherapy in the past?"

"My wife and I went to a marriage therapist for a few sessions. She seems to think that I'm a little too angry but I guess I blew it by getting angry at the marriage therapist."

"That can happen, Rob, but if you stay with it you can sometimes work through the negative transference, as we call it, and be freed of whatever is going on. It's all part of the therapeutic process. We better keep our focus on you for the present and maybe we can get back to what's going on in the marriage at another time, okay?"

"Fine by me."

"How about any clinical hypnosis or self-hypnosis training?"

"Well, Abbot, one time in high school, I went to this place where there was a stage hypnotist and he had people up on the stage doing all kinds of crazy things—dancing around and running from imaginary animals, and being very amorous, etc."

"Rob, that's something which is completely unethical for someone with my background. The American Society of Clinical Hypnosis does not allow its members to use clinical hypnosis for entertainment purposes, or even for demonstrations unless it's to train other colleagues. But again, we don't want to go off on tangents, so tell me about your education."

"Well, Abbot, I completed high school and then got an associate degree in electronics and have been using that in my work for the past few years. I work on an assembly line, usually making radios, but sometimes televisions and other electronic gadgets. We have to move fast and I can usually keep up, but right now I'm too depressed and unfocused to do a good job. That's part of what got me to Doctor Johnson-Angelo's office."

"Okay, Thanks. Now, tell me if you were raised by both parents and then tell me a little about your home situation?"

"Yes, Doctor, I mean Abbot, it gets confusing in a situation like this."

"I understand, Rob, it happens all the time."

"Well, Abbot, I was raised by both of my parents and have a younger sister and a younger brother. Our home life was pretty ordinary, I guess. My father hated religion and my mother loved it. She was always at church and he was always trying to put up with it."

"Any history of abuse from either side of the fence, Rob, you know physical, emotional, sexual?"

"Nothing I would call abuse, Abbot."

"How about abusing alcohol or drugs, yourself or anybody in the family?"

"No drugs or alcohol. If I may add to my earlier response to your question about being abused or abusing, the closest I've come to abuse in my childhood was when I went through a period of torturing animals—throwing rocks at cats and birds and punching dogs. Strange things like that, but I grew out of it."

"That's good, Rob."

As the history unfolded, Francis became more and more disturbed, not only on a cognitive level, but also on an intuitive level, in his spirit. He wanted to get to the heart of the matter right away, and he knew in this case Therapeutic Touch might be the most efficient way to do that.

"Well, I know you were probably expecting a good deal of talking today, but I see that you're pretty down and I think a healing technique called Therapeutic Touch might be the quickest way to get you back on the road to good health again.

"That's fine by me, Abbot, I have seen a few articles in the newspaper about it and I'm open to whatever will help."

"Good news. You can just sit over there on that little bench and relax, okay?"

"Sure enough."

"Being on the bench exposes your back as well as the rest of you to my hands a little more easily than if you're sitting in a chair or lying down. I'll put on a little soothing music on the tape recorder. How about something oriental sounding?"

"You are the doctor, Abbot."

CHAPTER 25

"I was afraid that waiting room full of patients was going to riot when I slipped in before all of them. Thanks for the time, John."

"Thank you for coming, Chantal. I know this must be important."

"I'm going to play this tape for you and I want you to see if you recognize the voice. It's a caller on a talk show."

"Okay, sure thing."

John's face was washed with fear as he heard the caller say that his wife should be tied to a rock and drowned. Chantal looked at him intently.

"You know who it is, don't you, John?"

"No, of course not. What makes you say that?"

"I can see it all over you. You know who it is, don't you?"

"No, I don't. What's this all about? Are you saying I murdered my wife or know who did it?"

"I'm saying, John, that you are too guilty or frightened or something to letting your conscious mind be aware of what you know. There's a voice inside of you that you don't want to hear."

"Now you sound like Francis. He says there's something inside me that won't let me see."

"Seeing, hearing, it's all the same at this level. Open up."

"I don't know how, Chantal. I admit that I think you're right. I have no rational reason for thinking that but I do and have been trying through meditation to open up."

"The breakthrough will come, John. It will come when you don't try quite so hard. There are lots of ways to get to the unconscious. Here, take this sheet of paper and this pencil and draw. Just draw for a few minutes while I play the tape of that voice over and over again."

John drew swirls and stars and trees and mountains, crosses, the Star of David, flowers, and then a car and a house—his house. The intensity of the moment produced a spontaneous trance in John and Chantal capitalized on it by speaking in a soothing monotone so as to access John's unconscious through the trance.

"Chantal, the person with that voice was sitting in this car the night Beth was murdered."

"And if you saw that and somehow didn't respond to that, you're probably feeling guilty and a victim of the distorted thinking cognitive psychologists call emotional reasoning. You feel that you caused her death so you can't admit that you even glimpsed somebody who later turned out to be a murderer. Do you know the person in the car, John, have you ever met him or her?

"Yes, I believe I have met him since that night, not before."

"Did you meet him socially, did you meet him in a restaurant, where do you think you met him, John?"

"I don't think it was socially, I think it was professionally. I met him here, I met him right where you are seated now. His name is Rob, Rob Williams. Chantal, am I responsible for my wife's death?"

"Of course not, John. Keep it together. We can process all of this later. Right now we've got to get hold of Dave. And you've got a waiting room full of patients to see."

"That's right. There's a small office down at the end of the hall. Why don't you go in there and see if you can get hold of Dave. Then let me know what's happening. I'll see my next person in the meanwhile. John left the room in what is sometimes called a "waking trance." He would function well with his patients, perhaps better than usual, since he was listening to himself and all of creation at such a deep level.

The dispatcher told Chantal that Dave was in the car out on the street and she would have him call her back rather than tie up the phone line at the doctor's office. Chantal went to John's receptionist and asked for the file of Rob Williams. The receptionist turned it over to her saying: "The doctor said to give you anything you want. I just hope it helps him."

Chantal went back to the small office at the end of the hall to wait for Dave's return phone call. She reviewed the chart and noticed that Rob had been in the Navy. As she was in the midst of reading about the sad death of Rob's daughter, the phone rang and startled her. She picked up the phone and heard Dave's voice say "What's up, little flower?"

"Plenty. I'm at John's office. He recognized the voice of one of his patients as being the caller on the talk show. We'd better check it out. The guy's name is Rob Williams. He was also in the Navy which ties us in to those fancy knots. Dave, the guy sounds kind of fragile. He's very depressed. His baby daughter died a few weeks ago. Maybe John should be with us when we question him."

"That makes a lot of sense Chantal. I have a few issues related to the case to take care of yet but I'll be over before very long and we can go together. How's that?"

"Sounds good, Dave. I'll read a few of the ancient magazines that are in the waiting room."

"John must be a good doctor if he has old magazines."

Chantal tried to make herself comfortable in the little office and waited for John's door to open so that she could talk to him about the plans she and Dave had made. Each minute seemed like an hour, and she began to feel like a patient waiting for a doctor. To keep herself focused and oriented, she had to remind herself that she was a doctor—a forensic psychologist—whose livelihood and way of contributing to the world was by dealing with issues like this. To calm herself and mobilize her energy Chantal started some deep breathing exercises and concentrated on a spot on the wall—a visual mantra to settle her soul and open her up to whatever there was out there that was running the universe. Chantal became unaware of her surroundings and found that her head was clearing when all of a sudden the door burst open and John came rushing in causing her body to lurch like an old rag doll."

"Chantal, I'm sorry that this is such a delayed reaction, but I just remembered that I referred Rob to Francis because of his depression and Francis agreed to see him. I don't know when they're meeting. We'd better get on the horn and see what's going on over at the monastery."

Chantal picked up the phone and quickly punched in the number. "No answer at Francis private number. There's a monastery number as well, John, but I don't know it by heart. I'll let my fingers do the walking and flip through the Yellow Pages. Here we are, listed under Convents and Monasteries, Salesian Monastery." Chantal punched in the numbers as John called them out. "It's another tape, John. This one saying when the hours of their common prayer are."

"Where the heck can everybody be over there? I have a feeling we better get there fast."

"Agreed. We'll take my car, John, if that's okay"

"No problem there. Let's go out to the waiting room first. I have some bad news to break."

"Ladies and gentlemen: I'm extremely sorry but there's a medical emergency and I have to leave now. I'm not sure when I'll be back. You can wait for me or have our very fine receptionist reschedule you. I'm sorry, I just have to go." And the two of them ran out the front door, leaving not only the patients but also the receptionist quite dazed.

As Chantal was pulling out from the curb, she pointed to the car phone between herself and John and said: "Please try to get hold of Dave and tell him what's happening. His number is in the memory of the phone, I think it's four."

John pushed four, and after a series of beeps the dispatcher from the Police Department answered. "This is Doctor Johnson-Angelo. It's imperative that I speak with Detective Gold."

"I'm sorry, Doctor, he's in the car and I believe en route to your office. I'll see if I can patch him through to you. Please hold."

"They're trying to connect us, Chantal."

Chantal seemed oblivious to everything but the road in front of her. An extremely goal-oriented woman, her goal was to get to the monastery and save Francis if he needed it. The dispatcher came on.

"Doctor, I haven't reached Detective Gold yet. He's probably some-where between his car and where he's going. I'm going to call his beeper and try to connect you two. Is there any message if I don't get you hooked up?"

"Yes, please tell him that Doctor Fleur and I are on our way to the monastery and that the killer might be there already."

"Very well, Doctor."

"What do you mean they're not here? I was supposed to meet Doctor Johnson-Angelo and Doctor Fleur here."

The receptionist said: "I'm sorry, Detective, I'm just as confused as you are. They didn't say where they were going either. That's so unlike the doctor. All they said was there was a medical emergency and they had to go."

"Did they leave any hint as to where they were going?"

"No, but they were in that little office in the back there, trying to contact someone or other. Maybe there's a name or number lying around."

Gold ran down the hall and looked around. No telephone numbers written on anything. The room was sparse and neat. He saw the Yellow Pages opened up. He scanned the pages for help. He began with Contractors and then moved into Control Systems, Convenience Stores, Convention Information Bureaus, and then he spotted it. Convents and Monasteries. They were on their way to the monastery.

CHAPTER 26

Francis was confused. He certainly didn't like the energy he was picking up. He felt a powerful surge of darkness and light, good and bad. It was as if a war were going on somewhere nearby. And then there was a sense of breaking through the shield that was around Rob, and Francis understood everything, like a zen *satori*, in one blinding moment.

With that experience of breakthrough, an audible crackle filled the air. Rob jumped up and ran out into the waiting room. Francis hesitated a moment, startled and dazed, and then ran out after him. A lightning bolt of electricity ricocheted through his brain as the Abbot fell to the floor in response to the rock which hit him in the occipital region of the back of his head.

"It's time for a second baptism, Abbot. It's the only way to clean you up," said the young man as he placed a noose around the unconscious monk's neck. The blond hair of the Baptist gleamed in the sun and his eyes glazed over as he dragged the abbot back through his office, out the office door, down steps, and to the front of the trailer where there was a meditation garden made up of a few benches bushes and flowers, with a circular pond about fifteen feet in diameter in the middle.

"I'm sure that you've gotten a lot of your insight and spirituality by sitting here and praying and now you will experience the ultimate—death and rising for the last time."

Chantal and John had gotten stuck on Route 80 West. Neither of them could think straight at this point. They sat for a few minutes trying to collect themselves when they heard the siren coming closer and closer. They turned to look and saw a police car, red and blue lights flashing, coming along the shoulder of the highway.

"Here we go again," she hollered to John. "This is the drill. We put on the flashers, keep this car unlocked, and get into Dave's car."

Before they knew it, they were in Dave's car and moving along the shoulder of the highway at a fast clip and then on to Route 209 South. The journey seemed endless. The three of them were testy with each other. Finally they were driving up the driveway to the monastery. Gold, followed by Chantal, followed by John, ran across the lawn and into the Abbot's office. The door was wide open and the energy was palpably negative.

"Something's terribly wrong," Chantal said, stating the obvious. Francis would never leave his office open with progress notes lying openly on his desk and the filing cabinet unlocked. Let's try the main building."

Once inside, Gold ran up the stairs in the main building, checking rooms. Chantal ran into the library which was empty except for the wisdom of the ages lining the shelves, and John hollered down a basement door. The place was deserted.

Dave barked orders: "We need to check every corner of the grounds. Chantal please walk up and down the far third of the property around the trailer—front and back. John, please go to the opposite end of the property, up and down the driveway, looking in the weeds on either side, and I'll examine the grounds, front and back, of the main house.

"What are we looking for?" John asked.

"A body, and I hope we're not lucky."

Chantal walked past the trailer and saw two long marks in the dirt and grass as if something had recently been dragged across the lawn. "Maybe I've been watching too many mystery movies," she thought to herself, "but I might as well follow the marks and see if they take me anywhere."

The trail ended near a bunch of shrubbery and it was then that she caught a glimpse of a blond head blending in with the tall faded brown weeds. She quietly walked closer and heard Scripture being recited.

"The Lord is my shepherd, I shall not want…I am the resurrection and the life. Whoever believes in me will never die."

"Where is he?" she screamed. "Where is he? What have you done with him?"

The blond head turned slowly and said: "He's died and risen for the last time and now he's where he needs to be—with his God."

She screamed so loudly that the other two came running to see what was going on. In the meanwhile, she ran into the pond and felt around with her arms and legs until she found the lifeless lump which she started pulling to the surface. Her two friends were in the pond lifting the burden along with her almost immediately. The three of them were barely able to drag the monk on to shore.

John hollered: "Wait, there's a rope around his neck; it's choking him." They pulled the end of the rope up and found a rock of about twenty pounds in weight. John released the noose from Francis's neck and began pushing on his chest to expel water. The boy was nowhere to be seen but Dave wasn't too worried. They had his name and description and would be able to pick him up easily. He went over to the Abbot's office to call the station for back-up and to get the information out on the street. First he dialed 911 for an ambulance.

As he put down the phone Chantal walked through the door whereupon they simultaneously heard what sounded like a knocking on the floor in the next room. Dave drew his gun and Chantal got behind a chair. The rapping continued. Dave hollered through the door, what do you want?

A weak voice responded: "Help me, help me." Dave cautiously opened the door and found a young blond man sprawled out on the floor, bleeding from the back of his head.

"What the…?" Dave said.

Chantal was behind him. "That's what I was coming in to tell you, Dave. Rob Williams was not the guy we saw outside. They just look a bit alike. The guy standing at the pond was the one you met at the church after that Miss Von Kiel from the Center for Traditional Catholicism gave you his name and address."

"Okay, okay, we'll sort it all out. Let's get some help here." In the background they could hear an ambulance screaming.

John rode in the ambulance with the now conscious abbot, uneasy about the possibility of brain damage since Francis had been under water for God knows how long. Dave was out on the streets looking for the perpetrator and Chantal remained at the monastery in order to fill in the community about the events whenever they returned from wherever they were. She took the liberty of rummaging in a hall closet and found a gray tunic and a towel and washcloth. After a warm shower she threw her clothing in a washer in the basement and, garbed in the tunic, sat drinking a cup of herb tea at the kitchen table.

Rob was treated and released from Pocono Medical Center. He had a laceration in the back of his head which was stitched up and was told to stay awake all night and have somebody in the house with him. His head pulsed with pain but his spirit was relieved that he was still alive.

Francis' headache subsided when he mentally bathed himself in clear light and focused on the negative energy draining from his body through his feet. He had a large "egg" on the back of his head and spent that day and a good bit of the days thereafter following fingers and lights with his eyes and being poked and prodded by physicians.

Eyes resting, Francis lay on his hospital bed thinking about the monastery he had to run and the patients he needed to see and in walked a priest from St. Matthew's, the local parish community which served the hospital.

"Well, this is a reversal of roles," said the jovial dark-complected cleric. "I've been coming to you for spiritual direction for about five years now and it's finally my turn to minister to you. What can I do for you?"

"Get me out of this place, Tony."

"Wait a minute, Francis, I seem to remember a lot of talk about abandonment, God's providence, and living in the present moment."

"I am doing all of that, but the lower part of my soul still wants me out of here. Now that I've said my piece, I will continue working on abandonment."

"That's just what you taught me, Francis, and it's nice to see it in action, humanity and spirituality working together for the good of the person and the good of the hospital."

"Get out of your pulpit, Tony."

"I'll do better than that—I'll get out of the room. I'll do what I can to get you released. Take care my faithful friend."

"You should have seen the looks on the faces of your community members when they came in from their day of playing and praying at the state park to find yours truly sitting at the kitchen table in a monastic tunic," Chantal said.

"I'm sure it livened the place up," Francis laughed. "I'll bet it really stripped old Benedict's gears."

"Yes, but he's always a perfect gentlemen. He said something like: 'may I get you something for your feet, Dr. Fleur?' And Sister Scholastica was so grateful that you were being taken care of by Doctor Johnson-Angelo. It seems that she went to him a few times prior to entering monastic life and really likes him."

Dave interrupted. "All right you two, enough of this rowdy behavior. The doctor said I could fill you in on a few more details, Francis, so here goes. Our friend, Mark Wilson, went over the Delaware Water Gap bridge into New Jersey, always a dangerous thing to do—hope no one here is from Jersey, after his little visit to the monastery. A forest ranger called the State Police after observing him standing on the banks of the Delaware and hollering obscenities at God for about a half hour. Extradition is pretty easy; he's on his way back now even as we speak."

Francis' clinical mind began to process the recent events: "The poor guy was so caught up in the superficialities of religion that he became paranoid and killed Beth, seeing her as a threat to religion. When that didn't solve his internal conflicts and make the world and the Church better, he must have thought that killing someone from the other end of the spectrum would do it, and thus Father Theophane met his demise. I suppose I was symbolic of the whole spectrum. How does it go, something old, something new."

"Let's see if I learned my psychology of religion well. Wilson is indiscriminately pro-religious, but tends to be extrinsically or letter of the law oriented," queried Dave.

"Sounds accurate to me," added Chantal, "although I think it's a bit more complex than that."

"Yes," Francis thought out loud, "there is probably a dual diagnosis here—perhaps borderline personality disorder, which often begins in early adulthood, exacerbated by his religious or spiritual problem, to use the DSM IV diagnosis. Not that the insurance carriers would care."

"Okay Doctor, I give up, tell me about borderline personality disorder," the detective said with an amused sigh.

"Borderline people have great difficulty with identity. They don't know where they end and others begin emotionally. Thus, they can become very paranoid and fearful of abandonment, projecting their hang ups on to others and believing that others think of them negatively, when it is often their own low self concept at work. Some will try to achieve identity by joining a group and vicariously becoming someone. Cult members are of this sort. Mark Wilson was probably trying to find his identity through the Church. When he perceived it as threatened, so was he. That is the reason I am so convinced that we need to live by what we believe, not by what we call ourselves, how we dress, what groups we belong to, even though those groups can be of great help to us when we allow them to serve us and we avoid becoming a slave to them. Enough for now, Dave?"

Before Dave could respond, in walked a perky, healthy-looking young lady in white. "Time for the abbot's massage."

"I'm not sure what this has to do with anything, folks, but I'm going to take advantage of it while I can. I think maybe John was just doing a good deed when he ordered this."

Francis and Matthew sat at the water's edge. The bright fall sun reflecting off of the pond made their faces shimmer and brisk air invigorated them.

"The nightmares really have stopped this time, Abbot. I'm getting to know a whole new side of myself."

"Does your anima have a name yet?"

"At first she wouldn't tell me her name; she was mad at me for not paying attention to her, for being afraid of her, for not letting her help me. Eventually, she confided in me that her name is Dawn."

"How beautiful," mused Francis. "Dawn brings light to our day and the anima brings light to our inner being. Matthew, we've got to face the things that frighten us and make friends with them so that we can become whole. On a psychological level, we might say we need to get rid of our defense mechanisms; on a spiritual and monastic level we might say that we need to grow in purity of heart."

"Is that why you're sitting here by the water, Abbot? You were almost murdered on this very spot and yet you seem so serene as you sit with me."

"I didn't think about it on a conscious level, Matthew, but, yes, I'm certain that my inner wisdom drew me here for that reason."

"Speaking of wisdom, I think I see Dr. Fleur making her way through the weeds. I'll let you two talk. Thank you for your time."

"Thank you for telling me how you're doing, Matthew. I'm sure all will be well."

"Don't let me disturb you guys," Chantal said as she appeared through the foliage like a doe after her young. "I can take a walk for a while."

"Well, I was just leaving, Dr. Fleur," said Matthew. "I know that the Abbot's in good hands now that you're here." The overgrown boy was becoming a man.

"Please have a seat," said Francis.

Chantal began: "You know me, Francis. I need to plunge right in, okay?"

"Surely, my friend. Why change at this point in your life?"

"I still can't figure out what made Rob come to your office for an appointment at that time and what made our murderer lurk around at exactly the same time. The timing of those events pulled the whole thing together and helped us to catch the real murderer."

"Some people call that 'synchronicity.' Remember that from graduate school, Chantal?"

"Yes, I do, Francis, but I never quite understood it."

Francis spoke slowly and prayerfully, as if he were listening to an inner voice. "You see there's a cosmic or spiritual time that's much different from our time and it has to do with the convergence of events, not the hands on a clock fashioned by our human minds and hands."

"Mmmm, I'm beginning to remember it a little. Something like you once told me about oriental medicine. We have a nervous system that we all talk about and can see and can dissect and we have a whole other nervous system of energy that is less visible to the eye. Our Eastern brothers and sisters talk about energy meridians and chakras and the like."

"Exactly, my good friend."

"Buy why did John think the person in the car outside his home the night Beth was murdered and the voice of the radio caller on the tape was Rob Williams, Francis? I still don't understand that."

"John has a lot of potential for the gift of intuition which I believe the Holy Spirit gives to each of us according to her own desires and plan, but John has not learned to use it very well yet. It takes much practice. Besides, there was so much happening on a spiritual level at one time in his life that he probably just got his signals crossed, so to speak. Interpreting the information received is an art. I always offer my impressions very tentatively and see how people respond. Once John opened up to this process, he began trying too hard. It gets in the way. But don't miss the most wonderful part. John's 'misinformation' saved my life and society is being protected from a very disturbed young man and hopefully he will find peace as well. The interpretation of the superficial or accidentals of the situation was inaccurate, to speak philosophically, but the substance was right on target, dead center—time, place, the whole deal. I am grateful."

Chantal continued, thinking out each word as she spoke. "Rob felt some kind of a deep connection with you at some point, probably when you were doing Therapeutic Touch. He felt as if you had penetrated his very soul. That experience flipped him out. He got so frightened he just got up and ran out of the room into the waiting room and there Mark Wilson hit him over the head with the rock to get him out of the way."

"That's right, Chantal. And then I went out to see what was going on and that's when I got clobbered. Ouch!"

"Ouch is right! I am so grateful that I saw those scuff marks in the dirt and grass, Francis, and that I could follow the marks over to the meditation pond. Another minute or two and things could have been very different. You've been given a clean bill of health, Francis. The doctors said that because you were healthy, a runner, you meditate, you eat right and practiced Therapeutic Touch on yourself going into this trauma you had a better prognosis for getting over it unscarred."

"Yes, that's another part of oriental medicine—do as much prevention as you can. Shortly before all of this happened, Chantal, I had an especially keen sense that something was about to break. While I was taking Rob's history, and a lot more strongly during Therapeutic Touch, I had profound sense of darkness and light, a split right down the middle of the personality, but I was very confused. It didn't seem to be coming from Rob. I couldn't understand what was going on. It must have been coming from Mark Wilson in the waiting room.

That experience was so powerful that it kind of clogged my perception of Rob, but eventually I broke through and had a sense of a lot of old hurt and pain that Rob needed to let go of and that his prognosis was pretty good if he would work with forgiveness and inner healing through journaling and meditating and the like. I got that information in a split section but as soon as it happened he was up off the bench and out into the waiting room."

"I am honored that you shared that personal experience with me, Francis, but there's still something else, isn't there?"

"Well, yes, I hesitate to talk about it because I don't understand it myself yet. My concept of God and my prayer have been changing since the beginning of this year. I took a little updating on Therapeutic Touch at the beginning of the year and since then I've met one person after another, either from the Orient or who's practicing some Eastern form of meditation. Books have been coming my way about it, and now I feel like when there's an extreme need I am getting some extra help."

"You mean like from God, Francis?"

"Well, God has always been helping. It's some other thing that's happening, though. When people experience intuitive information, Chantal, sometimes it's through an inner sense without words, or pictures, or anything at all sense related. Some people get pictures. Some might even hear words. I usually have an inner sense. I've lately been seeing a color as well—a beautiful orange that seems to be aflame or aglow, that seems to be boosting or supporting or adding to my connection with the cosmic Christ."

"That's another thing! Speaking of orange, Francis, last week when you were at the hospital and I was here waiting for the community to return so I could try to make some sense of what happened to you to the group, this little man appeared at the door, and I do mean appeared. I didn't even know he was there and then I heard the doorbell ring. He was dressed in orange robes and his brown hair was shoulder length. He had a deep resonant voice and a gentle smile, plus a name as long as an eye chart. Believe it or not, I was more curious than afraid so I went to the screen door and spoke with him. I didn't even unlock the screen door. He asked for Brother Francis and I said that you weren't in at this time.

He said: "Thank you sister, I was just coming to see how he is doing."

I said: "I'm not a nun but Abbot Francis has had some difficulty and is in the hospital at the moment."

Then the man said: "I know you're not a nun, I meant sisters, in the broadest sense of that word since we are all brothers and sisters and I know that you have a special relationship with Brother Francis."

And then he said to me: "I am sure our Brother will be fine. Please be at peace. And he walked away."

I stood there not knowing what to say but feeling a profound peace that I still can't explain and I knew with great certitude that you would be well. I think how I knew at that time is how you know things at times."

"Yes, it is knowledge understood at a deeper level. Thank you for telling me that, Chantal. That confirms issues a little bit for me."

Dave had a sense of meeting Mark Wilson somewhere before. Could that have been a little advance warning?"

"Very possibly, Chantal. I've still got some praying to do on the matter."
"I'll be going, Francis, and leave you to your prayer."
"Enjoy the rest of the day, Chantal, and thanks for everything."
"I certainly will enjoy it, Francis, I have a date." And off she skipped.
Francis sat there quietly for a long time and then as the brilliant orange of the sun gleamed on the pond he took off his sandals and habit and waded into the life-giving water.

Om, shanti, shanti, shanti.

ABOUT THE AUTHOR

Brother Bernard Seif, SMC, EdD, IABMCP is a Catholic monk, Clinical Psychologist, Diplomate in Behavioral Medicine, and Chinese medicine doctor specializing in medical qigong and Chinese medicinal herbs.

9 780595 174713